'Well for good
you going to sa

'Apologise or some
least you could do is get off your idle
backside and let me in! I'm soaked to the skin
and you don't give a damn.'

God, she was beautiful, with her hair a wild
tangle of damp curls and steam coming out of
her ears! Her eyes were spitting green sparks,
and her mouth when she finally paused for
breath was soft and lush and too wide for
conventional beauty, but he could imagine it
trailing over his poor wounded body and
kissing it better. He stifled a groan and met
her furious eyes.

'You're late. Help me up,' he said gruffly, and
she stopped in her tracks.

'Excuse me?'

'The ladder slipped. I think my arms are
broken. Could you please help me up?'

Her jaw flapped for a moment, and her eyes
widened, tracking over him and filling with
horror. 'Well, why on earth didn't you *say* so,
instead of just sitting there?'

Caroline Anderson's nursing career was brought to an abrupt halt by a back injury, but her interest in medical things led her to work first as a medical secretary and then, after completing her teacher training, as a lecturer in Medical Office Practice to trainee medical secretaries. She lives in rural Suffolk with her husband, two daughters and assorted animals.

Recent titles by the same author:

A MOTHER BY NATURE
GIVE ME FOREVER
JUST A FAMILY DOCTOR
MAKING MEMORIES

RESCUING
DR RYAN

BY
CAROLINE ANDERSON

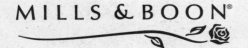

*First published in Great Britain 2001
Harlequin Mills & Boon Limited,
Eton House, 18-24 Paradise Road, Richmond, Surrey TW9 1SR*

© Caroline Anderson 2001

ISBN 0 263 82655 4

*Set in Times Roman 10½ on 12 pt.
03-0401-45173*

*Printed and bound in Spain
by Litografia Rosés, S.A., Barcelona*

CHAPTER ONE

'AH, NO!'

Will rammed his hands through his hair and stared disbelievingly at the wide, wet stain on the mattress. Cocking his head a little, he looked up at the ceiling, and winced. Yup, there was a corresponding stain, right over the middle of the bed. The new bed.

Great. There must be a missing tile on the roof, just over the bedroom, and, of course, as luck would have it, it had been the wettest March on record.

He sniffed experimentally, and sighed. Mildew. Lovely. Probably soaked right through the bed and rotted the carpet underneath. He said something his grandmother wouldn't have understood, and stomped out, slamming the door behind him.

Before anyone could use the little cottage, it would need a new bed—another one—and a new carpet—and Lucie Compton, their new GP registrar, was due in two hours. He crossed the yard, turned and squinted up into the sun. Yes, there it was—or wasn't. A neat hole in the middle of the roof slope. Still, it could have been worse. The tile was sitting in the gutter and hadn't smashed on the ground—although if it had smashed at least he would have stood a chance of noticing it sooner.

He gave a hefty sigh and fetched the ladder and some tools from the barn. Within moments he'd put the tile back and secured it, and checked the others around it. All looked fine.

Good. He put the tools away and came back for the ladder, and as he carried it round the end of the little converted barn he noticed Minnie, the tiny little Siamese kitten, running across the roof and crying.

'Oh, Minnie, how did you get up there?' he asked, exasperated.

'Mreouw—rrr,' she replied.

'Did you? Well, that'll teach me to leave the ladder there for you, won't it?'

'Mreow.'

'OK, I'm coming,' he said. He glanced at his watch. One hour seventeen minutes and counting. Hell.

He stuck the ladder up against the side of the barn, checked that it was steady and gave the sloping ground a dubious look. Oh, dammit. He didn't have time to tie it. He rattled it again, just to make sure it was secure, and climbed carefully to the top.

'Come on, Minnie. Come here.'

The kitten came almost within reach, sat down and cried piteously.

'Well, come here, then!' he coaxed with the last shred of his patience. He held out his fingers and she brushed against them. If he could just reach out...

The ladder jolted, lurching slightly to the side, and he grabbed the rungs and hung on, freezing for a moment.

Hmm. Now what? Minnie came to the top, within reach, and rubbed herself against the top rung. 'Damn cat,' he said with affection, and reached for her cautiously.

There was another lurch, and he felt the ladder sliding out from under him. He grabbed the top rung and prayed, but God was either elsewhere or had decided it was time Will was taught a lesson.

It was, he thought with strange detachment, almost like watching something in slow motion. The ladder skidded, dropped below the guttering and then slid down the side of the barn, gathering speed as it neared the ground.

Oh, hell, he thought. I really don't need this.

Then he hit the deck.

Everything hurt. His head hurt, his legs hurt, his ribs felt crushed, but it was his arms that were really, really giving him stick.

He rested his forehead on the rung in front of him and instantly regretted it. He shifted, finding a bit that wasn't bruised, and lay still for a moment, waiting for his chest to reinflate and his heart to slow down.

He was also waiting for the pain to recede, but he was a realist. Five minutes later his breathing and heart rate were back to normal, and he decided that two out of three weren't bad. Given a choice, he would have gone for a different two, of course.

The kitten rubbed herself against his head, and he cracked open an eye and glared at her balefully.

'I am going to kill you,' he said slowly and clearly. 'Just as soon as I work out how to get out of here.'

Unabashed, she sat down just inches away and washed herself.

Will ignored her. He had other problems more immediate than a bit of cathartic blood-letting. He shifted experimentally, and gasped. OK. Not a good idea to press down on his right arm. What about the left?

Nope.

Knees? Better. And shoulders were OK. Now, if he could just roll over...

He bit back a string of choice epithets, and rolled onto his back, falling with a sickening jolt to the ground beside the ladder.

Phase one completed. Now all he had to do was get to his feet, go inside and call for help.

Hah!

He lifted his head a fraction, and stifled a groan. Damn. Headache. He persisted, peering at his arms which lay awkwardly across his chest.

No doubt about the right one, he thought in disgust. He'd be lucky to get away without pinning and plating. And the left?

His wrist was swelling before his eyes, and if it got much bigger his watch was going to cut off the circulation to his hand. Wonderful. He closed his eyes with a sigh and laid his head back down carefully on the ground. He'd just have to wait for Lucie Compton to arrive and rescue him.

There was a lump of something hard sticking into his spine, but it was beyond him to shift himself away from it. It was just one more small pain amongst many. If he were a philosopher, he'd welcome the pain as proof that he was alive. However, he wasn't, and at that particular moment he wouldn't have minded being dead.

And then, just as if survival itself wasn't a big enough bundle of laughs, he felt the first heavy splash of rain hit his face....

Lucie was late. Lucie was usually late, but she really, really hadn't needed Fergus giving her the third degree on the way out.

He *knew* she had to do this, *knew* that spending time in a general practice was part of her GP training, *knew* that it was only temporary.

Well, not any more. Not the separation, at any rate, although her sojourn into the countryside would be as brief as she could get away with. Six months tops. That, on top of the six months she'd already spent in her inner-city practice, would see her qualified to practise as a GP, and then she'd be back in the city like a rat out of a trap.

Of course, she didn't *have* to spend the time in the country. She could quite easily have found another London practice but, to be honest, Fergus was one of the reasons she'd wanted to get away, at least just for a while, to put some distance between them and see if what they had was a forever thing or just a temporary habit that needed breaking.

Well, she'd broken it, in words of one syllable.

YOU DO NOT OWN ME. GO AWAY. LEAVE ME ALONE.

OK, mostly one syllable. He'd understood, anyway. He'd flounced off, slamming the door of his car and roaring off into the sunset—except it had been some time after sunrise and he hadn't roared anywhere very much in the traffic off the Fulham Road.

She pulled over to the side of the road and checked her map. It was raining, of course, blurring everything and making it harder to read the signs.

'"Pass the turning to High Corner and take the next track on the right. Follow to the end. It's a bit rough in places." Hmm.' She peered at the sandy track ahead. Could that be it? It didn't seem to have a sign, and looked like nothing more than a farm track, but the address was Ferryview Farm, so it was possible.

With a resigned shrug, she turned onto the track and followed it. Some of it was sandy, some stony, some just downright boggy. It *was* a bit rough in places, she thought, and then lurched into a pothole.

Make that very rough, she corrected herself, and picked her way carefully through the next few puddles. Of course, without the rain—

There was a lurch, a nasty crunching grinding noise and her car came to rest on the centre of the track, its wheels dangling in matched potholes.

She put it in reverse and tried to drive out, but it was stuck fast, teetering on a high point. Damn.

Damn, damn, damn.

She got out, straight into a puddle that went over her ankle, and slammed her car door with a wail of frustration. Just let Dr Ryan wait until she caught up with him!

Pulling her coat close around her shoulders and hitching the collar up against the driving rain, she headed up the track. It couldn't be far, surely?

Not that it mattered if it was miles. She had no choice, not until she could get a breakdown truck to come and drag her car off the track.

Always assuming, of course, that she hadn't shattered the sump!

'Look on the bright side, Lucie,' she told herself, scraping a muddy hand through her rapidly frizzling hair. 'It could be snowing.'

Ten seconds later a little flurry of sleet plastered itself against her face. 'I didn't say that!' she wailed, and hitched the collar higher. The moment she caught up with Dr William 'it's a bit rough in places' Ryan, she was going to kill him!

She was late. Typical bloody woman, she was late, just when he needed her. He thought again of struggling to his feet and trying to get inside, but after the effort of sitting up and shuffling back into the lee of the barn, he thought it would probably kill him. Besides, the house keys were in his pocket, and he knew getting them out was beyond him.

So he sat, and he waited, and he fumed.

Still, he had Minnie for company—Minnie, the cause of all his grief. He might have known the damn cat was perfectly capable of getting herself down off the roof. If he'd thought about it at all, which, of course, he hadn't, he would have realised she could jump down on the top of the oil storage tank at the back and thence down to the ground. It was probably the way she'd got up in the first place.

He dropped his head back against the side of the barn and closed his eyes. The sun was out now—typical of April, sleet and driving rain one minute, glorious sunshine the next—and where he was sitting in the shelter of the barn, he was facing directly into it.

Good. It might warm him up, stop him shivering uncontrollably. He was in shock, of course, because of the fracture. Fractures? His right arm was certainly distorted, and his left was still swelling around the wrist. His watch was painfully tight, the flesh bulging each side of the broad metal strap. He tried to undo it with his teeth, but it was too firm and, besides, it hurt too much to prod about with it unnecessarily.

Please, God, don't let me have two broken arms,

he thought in despair. His mind ran through a list of things he couldn't do with two broken arms—and there were a lot in there that were very personal!

God again, teaching him compassion for his patients? Giving him a closer understanding of their needs and suffering?

Or just fate playing a nasty practical joke?

Where was Lucie Compton? Richard had waxed so lyrical about her after he'd interviewed her that Will had had great hopes—but if her medical skills were as good as her timekeeping, it didn't bode well for her patients. And he, he realised, was going to be her first one.

Hell.

Bruno was barking in the house, shut inside because Will had just been on his way out when he'd checked the cottage and found the leak. However, the dog had been quiet until now apart from the odd bark, and now he was letting loose with a volley. Someone coming?

Odd. Surely not Lucie? Will couldn't hear a car, but there was something. Footsteps. Fast, cross little footsteps.

A woman came into view, small, bedraggled and evidently as mad as a wet hen. She marched up to him, fixed him with a glare and said crisply, 'A bit rough in places?'

What? He opened his mouth to speak, but she rattled on, clearly divesting herself of some pent-up rage.

'I could have you up under the Trades Descriptions Act!' she stormed. 'A bit rough! Do you know I've grounded my car and probably trashed it on your damn drive?'

Oh, hell. It *was* Lucie Compton, finally. And now he'd get to test her medical skills, if he could just get a word in—

'I expect the sump's broken, knowing my luck,' she ranted on, 'and I'll have to get the engine replaced! And I'm wringing wet and frozen, and my mobile phone doesn't work out here in this God-forsaken bit of wilderness, and all you can do is sit there and smirk!'

She lifted her foot, and for a sickening moment he thought she was going to kick him, but she stamped it crossly and spun on her heel, walking away and then wheeling round and striding back.

'Well, for goodness' sake, aren't you going to say anything? Apologise or something? I mean, the very least you could do is get off your idle backside and let me in! I'm soaked to the skin, I'm freezing to death and you don't give a damn.'

God, she was beautiful, with her hair a wild tangle of damp curls and steam coming out of her ears! Her eyes were spitting green sparks, and her mouth when she finally paused for breath was soft and lush and too wide for conventional beauty, but he could imagine it trailing over his poor wounded body and kissing it better. He stifled a groan and met her furious eyes.

'You're late. Help me up,' he said gruffly, and she stopped in her tracks and her wide, soft, pretty mouth fell open in surprise.

'Excuse me?'

'The ladder slipped. I think my arms are broken. Could you, please, help me up?'

Her jaw flapped for a moment, and her eyes widened, tracking over him and filling with horror.

'Well, why on earth didn't you *say* so, instead of just sitting there?'

'I would have done, but you made it well nigh impossible to get a word in edgeways,' he said drily. To his satisfaction she coloured, the anger going out of her like air out of a punctured balloon.

'Sorry,' she conceded gruffly. 'Um…how do you suggest we do this? What have you broken?'

'Right radius and ulna, and maybe something in my left wrist. Oh, and I'm a bit concussed and my legs hurt like hell, but they move, at least. Otherwise I'm just peachy.'

'Right. Um.'

She crouched down and bent over him, the damp tendrils of her wildly curling hair teasing his face. 'May I see?'

He lowered his legs, wincing as he did so, and revealed his forearms. 'Don't touch anything,' he warned through gritted teeth, and she nodded. Thank God she only looked, and didn't feel the need to prod him.

'OK. You need a couple of slings before I try and move you. Have you got any in the house?'

'Yes, but until I get up you can't get in. The keys are in my pocket.'

'Oh.' She glanced down at his jeans, snug around his hips, and she coloured slightly. 'Um—are you sure? Which pocket?'

'The right.'

'You could shift onto your left hip and I could see if I could wriggle my hand in…'

He shifted, swallowing hard and hoping for a good hefty jolt of pain to take his mind off those slender little fingers. They wormed and wriggled their way in, while she blushed and apologised. She gave a little grunt of effort and her breath puffed soft and minty-fresh over his face. He closed his eyes and groaned, and wondered how long it would be before he embarrassed himself with her prodding and probing about so damn close—

'Got them!' she said victoriously, brandishing them in front of his nose.

He sighed with relief. 'Mind the dog. He's all right, but he'll come and jump all over me, and I don't need it just now.'

'I'll keep him in,' she promised. 'Where are the slings?'

'Kitchen. Cupboard on the left of the sink. The dog's called Bruno.' He watched her go, and wondered how, in the midst of so much pain, he could be so aware of her cute little bottom in those tight, unbelievably sexy jeans...

Lucie let herself in and greeted the dog, a huge hairy black thing with doleful eyes and jaws that could have sheared a man's thigh, and hoped the eyes would win.

'Good doggie, nice Bruno. Sit.'

To her amazement he sat, his tail wiggling furiously, and she reached out a tentative hand and patted him. 'Good boy,' she said, a little more confidently, and he barked again, standing up and going to the door to scratch hopefully at it.

'Sorry, babes, you've got to stay inside,' she told him, and looked around. Sink. Good. Cupboard on left—and slings. Excellent. She squirmed past the dog, shut the door and ran back down the steps and over to the barn.

His eyes were shut, and she could see, now she

was less angry, that his face was grey and drawn.
She wondered how long he'd been there, and how
on earth she'd get him out.

'Dr Ryan?'

'Will,' he mumbled, opening his eyes. 'Lucie, take
my watch off, can you? It hurts like hell.'

She carefully unclipped the metal strap, but she
couldn't slide it over his hand. The face was cracked,
and it had stopped about three hours ago. Had he
been there that long? Probably.

'Let's get a support on that right arm first,' she
said, and carefully lifted his hand as he shifted his
elbow away from his body.

She was as gentle as possible, but he still bit back
a groan and braced himself against the barn. She
fixed the sling, then put the left arm, which seemed
less painful, in a lower sling so it wouldn't interfere
with the right.

'OK. Now I need to get you up and out to hospital.
Any ideas?'

His eyes flickered open. 'Teleporting?'

Humour, even in all that pain. She felt a flicker of
admiration. 'Sorry, not an option. Do you have a
car?'

'Yes. It's round the corner in the barn. The keys
are with the door keys. Lock the back door again and
get the car out and bring it round.'

'What about insurance?' she asked, being practical
for once in her life.

'You're covered if you're over twenty-five.' He
gave her a sceptical look.

'Well, of course I am!' she said in disgust, and
stomped off. 'Idiot. He knows quite well how old I

am!' She locked the back door, ignoring Bruno's pleas, and went round the corner.

Oh, lord, it was a massive great Volvo estate! Miles long, and hugely wide. Terrific. She'd never driven anything this big before, and she was going to have to do it smoothly and carefully. With an audience.

Marvellous. She could hardly wait.

She got in, stared at the gear lever and got out again, stomping back round the corner to Will.

'It's automatic,' she said accusingly.

'Yes—that makes it easier.'

'Fiddlesticks.'

'Trust me, I'm a doctor. D is drive, P is park, R is reverse, N is neutral. Leave it in Park, start the engine, put your foot on the brake and put it into Drive. You have to hold down the button on top while you move the lever.'

'Hmm.'

She went back, started it, put it in drive and took her foot cautiously off the brake and screamed when it moved. She hit the brakes, her left foot flailing uselessly, looking for a task. Idiot, she told herself, and eased her foot off the brake again. It rolled gently forwards, and she tried the accelerator, cautiously. OK.

She nosed out of the barn, totally unsure how far she was from anything, and cursed herself for never having driven anything bigger than a supermini. She crept round the end of the barn, stopped as close to Will as she could get and looked at the gear lever in puzzlement.

'Put it in Park,' he told her. 'And put the handbrake on,' he added as an afterthought, as if he didn't quite trust her.

She was about to make a smart-alec retort when she took her foot off the footbrake and the car rolled forwards a fraction.

She gave another little yelp and slammed her foot back down, and he shot her a pitying look.

'It moved!' she said defensively.

'It's fine. It's just taking up the slack. You could have reversed it in so the door was closer.'

'No, I couldn't,' Lucie said tightly, realising with dismay that she was going to have to reverse around the barn to get back to the track. Oh, blast. She got out of the car and slammed the door, and he winced.

'Maybe this wasn't such a good idea,' he muttered.

'You don't have a choice,' she reminded him.

'We could have called an ambulance.'

'We might have to yet. My car's in the way.'

'I've got a tow-rope. We can pull it out.'

'We?' She eyed him up and down, and snorted. 'I don't think so.'

'We'll worry about it later. Just get me in the damn car,' Will said through gritted teeth, and she stood in front of him and grasped him by the shoulders, pulling him forwards and upwards as he got his legs under him and straightened with a groan.

'OK?'

He gave her a dirty look. 'Wonderful. Open the car door.'

She cocked an eyebrow at him. 'Please?'

'Please.'

'Better.'

'Don't push it,' he growled, and she gave up. She stomped round the bonnet, yanked open the front passenger door and came back for him, but he was already on his way, stubborn and self-reliant. Fine. Let him struggle.

Then Will wavered, and she had a sudden vision of him toppling over on those broken arms. Not a good idea, and she needed this post if she was going to finish her training. Stifling her urge to leave him to it, she put her arm around his waist to steady him and helped him round the car, then opened the door and watched as he eased himself in. His jaw was working furiously, his eyes were screwed shut and once he was in he dropped his head back against the headrest and let out a shaky sigh.

'I think we'll pass on the seat belt,' he said through gritted teeth, and she shut the door firmly on him.

Lucie crossed round to the driver's side, wondering how, under these circumstances, she could have been so conscious of the hard, lean feel of his body. Even through the thickness of the soft sweater he was wearing she'd been aware of every rib, every muscle, every breath.

She had a feeling he was, too, and her compassion returned, forcing out her bizarre and untimely thoughts and replacing them with a more appropriate concern for his health. She slid behind the wheel, looked over her shoulder and wondered how on earth she was going to reverse this thing the size of an oil tanker back around the barn...

How could she be so stupid? Will asked himself. How could a woman with apparently enough brain to train and qualify as a doctor be so stupid that she couldn't manage to drive a perfectly normal car?

She panicked, she overreacted, she allowed sometimes too much room, sometimes nothing like enough, and her judgement on the bumpy drive left a great deal to be desired.

No wonder she'd got her car stuck.

'Are you trying to do it again, you idiot woman?' he snapped as she jolted down yet another pothole.

'Don't call me names just because your drive's so awful! There should be a law against it.'

There should be a law against her smart mouth, but he didn't suppose he'd get it past all the women MPs. 'Drive on the centre and the side,' he told her through gritted teeth, but there were places where you had to pick your way and, sure as eggs, she'd pick the wrong one.

And every jolt was agonising. He would have driven himself, except, of course, he couldn't even hold the steering-wheel, never mind turn it. Damn.

They lurched through another pothole and he felt cold sweat spring out on his brow. He needed to lie down. He needed pain relief. He needed oblivion.

He didn't need to be giving some delinquent female driving lessons!

'There's my car,' she announced defiantly, and he cracked his eyes open and sighed with relief.

'You can drive round it. Head for the left—the ground's firm there.'

Well, more or less. They got through it with a bit of lurching and wheel-spinning, and then the track improved. Just another few minutes, he told himself. Just a little longer…

'Yes, it's a lovely clean fracture through the radius and ulna. Classic Colles'. We'll reduce it here, if you like. As for the other one, it's just a nasty sprain, you'll be glad to know.'

He was. He was hugely glad to know that he wasn't going to be dependent on anyone for help with his basic functions. It would probably hurt like hell to use it, but at least if it wasn't plastered, he'd have some rotation in the hand, and that would make all the difference.

Will didn't enjoy having the fracture reduced. They bandaged his hand to compress it and drive the blood out of it, which hurt, then stopped the blood supply to his arm and filled the vessels with local anaesthetic.

That bit was fine. Then the doctor grasped his hand and pulled, and the bones slid back into place with an audible crunch.

To his utter disgust, he threw up, and all he could think was thank God Lucie wasn't there watching him with her wide green eyes and sassy mouth. Just for good measure, he retched again, then sagged back against the bed.

'Finished?' the nurse asked him in a kind voice, and he nodded weakly.

The doctor shot him a thoughtful look. 'I think you've got a touch of concussion. Perhaps we need to keep you in overnight.'

'No,' he said firmly, ignoring the pounding in his head and the tingling sensation in his cheek. What concussion? 'I'm fine. I want to go home.'

'Stubborn sod, aren't you?' the doctor said cheerfully, and stood back to survey his handiwork. 'That looks fine. We'll let the anaesthetic out now and see how it feels when it comes round. Oh, and you'll need another X-ray after we put a back-slab on—an open cast, just in case it swells overnight. You'll need to come back tomorrow for a check-up and have a proper cast on if all's well. OK?'

Will nodded.

'I still think you should stay overnight, but so long as you'll have someone with you, that'll have to do. You know what to look out for.'

He did. He'd dished out advice on head injuries for years, but he'd never had to take it. He wasn't thinking too clearly now, and his hand was beginning to tingle as they let the blood back through it.

At least the other one felt safer now, strapped up and supported from his fingers to his elbow in tight Tubigrip with a hole cut for the thumb.

MICE, he was reminded. Mobilisation, ice, compression, elevation. It used to be RICE, but they'd changed the rules and got rid of the resting in favour of mobilisation. That was good, because without his right arm, the left was going to be mobilised a heck of a lot in the next few weeks!

'I'll write you up for some painkillers,' the doctor said. 'You can take up to eight a day, no more than two at a time and no closer together than four hours.'

He had no intention of taking them, except as a last resort, but he accepted them anyway—not that it was exactly difficult to get a prescription. He'd pick one up on Monday morning when he went to work, he thought, and then it hit him.

How on earth was he going to work with one arm in a cast and the other—the wrong one—in a support? Brilliant. And Lucie was just starting a six-month stint as a trainee, and he was the only member of the practice qualified to train her.

He sighed. Well, she'd just have to cover his patients, and he'd supervise her and tell her what to do and she could drive him around—always assuming he could stand it! She'd be staying at the cottage anyway, he thought, and then remembered the cottage bedroom—the one without a bed, with a stinking, soaked carpet that needed replacing.

He let his breath out on an irritated sigh. She'd have to stay in the house—which might be as well for a day or two, but in the long term would drive him utterly frantic. Still, it wouldn't need to be long term. He could order a bed and a carpet over the phone, and have them installed and move her in there within a couple of days.

He would need to. He guarded his privacy jealously, and he wasn't sharing his house with anyone any longer than was absolutely necessary.

Most particularly not a pretty, sassy little thing with attitude. He'd lose his mind!

Lucie was bored. She'd read all the leaflets, studied all the posters, walked up and down all the corridors, tried out the drinks machine and read half the magazines.

How long could it take, she thought, to do a couple of X-rays and slap on a cast?

A nurse appeared. 'Dr Compton?'

Finally! She bounced to her feet and crossed the room. 'How is he?'

The nurse smiled understandingly. 'Bit grouchy. Men don't like losing their independence. He's ready to go home now.'

Lucie followed her to one of the treatment rooms, and there was Will sitting in the wheelchair, looking like something the cat had dragged in. He shot her a conciliatory look. 'Sorry you've had such a long wait.'

'That's OK. I know more than I ever wanted to know about how to sail the Atlantic, adjust grand-father clocks and make mango chutney. Do you want a wheelchair ride to the car, or shall I bring it to the door?'

'Both,' the nurse said.

'I'll walk,' said Will.

Lucie looked from one to the other, nodded and went out, jingling the car keys in her hand and hum-ming softly, a smile playing around her lips. Stub-born, difficult man. It was going to be an interesting six months.

CHAPTER TWO

'WHAT do you mean, *uninhabitable*?'

Will sighed and shifted his right arm, swore softly and dropped his head back against the wall behind his chair. Lucie had got the distinct impression he'd been about to ram his hand through his hair in irritation. 'There was a missing roof tile. That's what I was doing.'

'You said you were rescuing the cat,' she accused, and he sighed again, even more shortly.

'I was—she'd gone up there because I'd been up there, fixing the roof. Because it was leaking. So the bed was wet. The carpet's ruined. The room is trashed, basically, until I can get a new carpet and bed next week and get the ceiling repainted.'

So not too long to wait, then. Just a few days of each other's company. It might be just as well, the state he was in. Lucie cocked her head on one side and studied Will. He looked awful. She wondered when he was going to relent and have a painkiller. Never, probably.

Stubborn as a mule.

He opened his eyes and looked at her, then looked at the door and dragged in a deep breath. Then he got very slowly and carefully to his feet.

'Can I get you something?'

'I need the loo.'

She went to stand up, and he fixed her with a glare that would have frozen the Atlantic. 'Don't even think about it,' he said tautly, and, suppressing a smile, she fell back in the chair and waited patiently for him to return.

Buttons, Will decided, were the spawn of the devil. Desperation got them undone. Nothing seemed sufficiently urgent to induce him to hurt that much just to do them up. Lord knows why he'd bought button-fly jeans. He must have been mad. So now what? Flies undone, or change into something more sensible, like tracksuit bottoms?

But they were upstairs, and he was down here, and it was all too much like hard work. His head was spinning, and he felt sick again. Damn. He tried to turn the tap on, but the washer needed changing and he always had to turn it off hard to stop it dripping. The other tap might be better.

Apparently not. It wouldn't budge for the feeble urging of his left hand, and his right was totally out of action.

He leant his head against the wall and winced as he encountered a bruise. If he'd been three, he would have thrown himself down on the floor and wailed, but he wasn't. He was thirty-three, and stubborn and proud, and he wasn't giving Lucie the privilege of seeing him this far down.

'Will? Are you OK?'

'Fine,' he lied through clenched teeth.

'I thought you might want these jogging bottoms—I found them on the chair in your bedroom. They'll be more comfortable to slouch around in, I should think.'

He opened the door—thank the Lord he had levers, not knobs—and took them from her. The damn

woman must be psychic. He avoided her eyes. He
didn't want to see mockery or, worse still, pity in
them. He pushed the door shut with his hip.

Her voice came muffled through the wood. 'Thank
you. My pleasure, any time. You're too good to me,
Lucie. No, no, not at all.'

'Thank you,' he bit out tightly, and looked at the
trousers, then at his feet. All he had to do now was
get his shoes off and swap the trousers without falling over.

Will looked awful. Grey and drawn and sick. He'd
been ages just changing into the jogging bottoms,
and now he was slumped in a chair in his cheerless
little sitting room while she struggled to light the fire.

Finally it caught, and Lucie put a log on the kin-
dling and prodded it. It spat at her out of gratitude,
so she put another log on to keep it company and
put the spark guard in front.

Bruno seemed to approve. He gave a deep grunting sigh as he collapsed in front of it, and proceeded
to sleep. It was what Will needed to do, of course,
but he was fighting it.

'Why don't you go to bed?' she suggested after an
hour of watching him wrestle with his eyelids.

'I need to stay awake—concussion,' he told her in
a patronising tone that made her grind her teeth.

'No, you need to be monitored so you don't go
into a coma without anyone noticing. I can do that—
I am almost qualified to tell if a person's alive or
dead, you know.'

He gave her a baleful look and shut his eyes again.
'I'm fine.'

Like hell he was fine, but who was she to argue?

Taking the suitcase with her overnight things, which they'd retrieved from her car, she went upstairs, found a bedroom next to his that was obviously a guest room and made the bed with sheets from the airing cupboard in the bathroom.

Once she'd done that, she went into his room, changed his sheets and turned back the bed. He'd need to sleep, whether he liked it or not, and she'd monitor him, again whether he liked it or not.

She went downstairs and stopped in front of him, studying him. He had dozed off, his head resting awkwardly against the wall, and for a moment she contemplated leaving him.

His eyes were shut, the lashes dark against his ashen cheeks, and his brows arched proudly above them. Most people looked younger and even innocent in sleep. Not Will. He looked hard and craggy and implacable. Tough. Indestructible.

Sexy.

Good grief. *Sexy?* She looked again. Well, maybe. He was probably quite good-looking, really, she conceded absently. Tousled mid-brown hair flopped in disorder over a broad, intelligent brow. Beneath it his nose was lean and aristocratic, despite the kink in it that gave away an old injury. Below the sculpted, full lips were a strong jaw and stubborn chin—no surprise there.

Sexy? Maybe. Certainly interesting in a strictly academic, architectural sense. And he did have beautiful, striking pale grey eyes brought into sharp relief by a darker rim. They weren't comfortable eyes. Too piercing. She wondered if they ever softened, if he ever softened.

Probably not.

They flickered slightly, but didn't open. He was awake now, though. She could tell. 'Will?' she said softly.

He opened them, spearing her with a surprisingly alert gaze. 'What?'

'Your bed's ready. Do you want anything to eat before you go to sleep?'

He sighed heavily. 'No. I feel sick still.'

'Water? You ought to drink plenty to help your kidneys deal with all the rubbish in your bloodstream after your fracture.'

He nodded. 'I know. I'll get some water in a minute.'

'How about painkillers?'

'Don't need them,' he said, a little too quickly.

'I'll get you some water, then I think you should go and lie down. You'll be much more comfortable.'

'Did anyone ever tell you just how damn bossy you are?' he growled.

'Mm-hmm. Lots of times,' she said cheerfully. 'Where does the dog sleep?'

'In here, now you've lit the fire, I should think. Anywhere. Usually outside my bedroom door.'

She went upstairs with the water and his painkillers, and came back for him, only to find him halfway up the stairs with that look on his face that brooked no interference.

She stood back and prayed he didn't fall backwards onto his stubborn behind, and once he was up she followed him to his room.

'I can manage,' he said, and she looked at him.

'Are there buttons on your shirt?'

He gave a short sigh of irritation. 'Yes.'

'Will, just for tonight, why don't you let me help you?' she suggested softly.

The fight went out of Will and he sat on the bed, looking at it in confusion. 'You changed the sheets.' His voice held astonishment and—heavens, gratitude? Surely not!

'I always think fresh sheets make you feel much better,' she said matter-of-factly. 'Right, let's get this sweater off and see if your shirt will come over the cast.'

It did, leaving him naked to the waist and utterly fascinating to her. His body was lean and muscled, healthy—and striped with purpling bruises from the rungs of the ladder. She touched his ribs with a gentle finger.

'You need arnica,' she told him, and he rolled his eyes.

'Not witchcraft,' he groaned.

She smiled. 'Midwives use it. You should open your mind.'

He humphed.

'Pyjamas?'

He shook his head slightly. 'No. I can manage now.'

'Socks?'

He looked at his feet, and his shoulders drooped. 'I can sleep in them.'

'Do you usually?'

'Of course not.'

'Fine.' Lucie crouched down and pulled off his socks.

Nice feet. Strong, straight toes, good firm arches, a scatter of dark hair over the instep.

'Now I really can manage,' he repeated, and she

stood up, putting the shirt and socks out of range so she didn't trip over them in the night.

'Water on the side. Can you hold the glass?'

'I'm sure I'll find a way,' he said drily.

'No doubt. OK, I'll see you later. I'm next door. Shout if you want anything.'

She got ready for bed and lay down, and the silence and darkness was astonishing. She looked out of the bedroom window, and could see nothing. No lights, no sign of any other habitation. Something scuttled in the roof over her head, and she ducked and ran back to bed. Her skin crawled with fear until she realised it was in the roof space and not in the room with her.

'It's probably a tiny little mouse,' she told herself, ignoring the vivid imagination that had always been her worse enemy as well as her greatest friend. That imagination was turning the mouse into a rat of terrifying proportions, and she had to force herself to relax. She buried her head under the pillow and then remembered she was supposed to be listening out for Will.

Damn. She poked her head out and listened.

Nothing. Well, nothing human. There was a snort right outside her window, and fear raced over her skin again. What on *earth* was that? She bit her lip, considering creeping into Will's room and sliding into bed next to him for safety, then dismissed it as ridiculous.

Whatever was out there was *out there*, not in here with her. She'd be fine. Fine. Fine.

She chanted it like a mantra, and eventually she drifted off into a light, uneasy doze…

*   *   *

He'd thought he'd be all right. He'd really thought the pain wouldn't keep him awake, but the hospital's painkiller had worn off well and truly, and his arm was giving him hell. Well, both of them, really, but especially the right.

Will sat up, swinging his legs over the side of the bed and waiting a moment for the world to steady. He didn't know where Lucie had put his painkillers, but he had a bottle in his medical bag downstairs that he kept for emergencies—other people's, not his, but they'd do.

He went down to the kitchen, creeping past Lucie's open door, and struggled with the combination lock on his bag. Finally he broke into it, pulled out the bottle and stared at it in disbelief.

A safety cap! Marvellous. He didn't know if he could turn it, never mind press and turn simultaneously. He tried holding the bottle in his right hand, but his fingers wouldn't co-operate. He held in it his left, and pressed with the cast to release the safety catch while he turned the bottle.

The cap slipped, of course, and was no further off. However, he still had teeth. He held the bottle to his mouth, clamped the cap in his back teeth and pushed and twisted.

Pain shot through his wrist, and with a gasp he dropped the bottle on the floor.

Damn. He'd never get into the blasted thing.

Bruno came to investigate, giving him a great, wet kiss as he bent to pick up the bottle. 'Hello, you vile hound,' he said affectionately, and could have buried his face in the dog's thick, black ruff and howled with despair.

Then he spotted the hammer on the window sill.

*   *   *

What on earth was Will doing? Lucie tiptoed to the top of the stairs and peered down. She could see his feet in the kitchen, and hear the occasional thump and groan. Then there was an almighty crash, and she ran downstairs and found him slumped over the sink.

'Will?'

He straightened slowly and turned, glaring at her. 'I can't get the bloody lid off,' he bit out through clenched teeth.

'And, of course, it's beyond you to ask for help.'

'I didn't want to wake you.'

'And you think all this crashing around right under my bedroom wouldn't have woken me, even assuming I'd been to sleep? Hell, it's too damn quiet round here to sleep, anyway! I can hear every mouse skittering in the roof, and birds shuffling in their nests, and some—some *thing* snorted outside my window. I nearly died of fright.'

'That would be Henry.'

'Henry?'

'A horse. He lives here.'

A horse? Of course. How obvious. She felt silly. She got back to basics. 'Where's the bottle?'

'Here.' He jerked his head at the worktop, and she picked the bottle up and studied it.

'These aren't the ones.'

'They'll do. I didn't know where the others were.'

'Beside your bed. I put two out.'

He closed his eyes and sighed harshly. 'Right. Fine. Thanks.'

'How's the nausea?'

'Gorgeous. I don't even know if I'll keep them down.'

'Yes, you will,' she said in her best comforting voice. 'Come on, let's get you back upstairs and into bed before you fall over. What was the crash, by the way?'

'The hammer.'

'*Hammer?*' she said in disbelief. 'What, did you think you'd tackle a few outstanding DIY jobs or something?'

He snorted in disgust. 'I was trying to break the bottle. I couldn't even hold the damn thing. It fell in the sink.'

Compassion filled her soft heart. 'Come on,' she said gently, putting an arm around his waist and steering him towards the stairs. 'Bedtime. I'll give you your painkillers and you can get to sleep.'

This time Bruno followed them, and with just the tiniest bit of encouragement he curled up across the foot of her bed and crushed her feet. She didn't care. She felt safe with him there, and she knew he'd hear every move that Will made. Finally able to relax, she went to sleep at last.

Will slept for most of the next day. Lucie took advantage of it to go and rescue her car. The puddles had more or less drained away, and she found some old bricks and put them in the back of Will's Volvo, then drove carefully—on the middle and the side— up to her car. She jacked it up, put bricks under the wheels and leading out of the puddle, then let the jack down and drove out.

No engine damage, or not obviously, and she'd done it herself. She felt disgustingly proud of her achievement, and couldn't wait to see Will's face. Leaving the bricks *in situ* to fill up the pothole a little, she headed back in her car, parked it in the yard beside the cottage and walked back for Will's.

By the time she drove back into the yard the second time, she was hot and sticky and Will was up.

'Where the hell have you been?' he asked crossly as she went into the kitchen.

'Well, pardon me for breathing! I fetched my car.'

He cobbled his eyebrows together. 'You did?'

'Yup. I found some old bricks at the side of the barn—'

'Bricks?'

'Yes—you know, rectangular red things that they build houses out of? Except these are dirty yellow and grey.'

'I know what you're talking about,' he snarled. 'I just wonder if you do! They were floor bricks—carefully cleaned and ready to go down in the kitchen here, once I had a minute. How many did you take?'

She shrugged, feeling a twinge of guilt. 'About forty or so?'

'*Forty!*' He rolled his eyes and gave an exasperated sigh.

Whoops.

'They'll clean up again,' she suggested. 'They only need a wash.'

'Good. You might go and fetch them and do it— and don't put them all covered in mud into the back of my car!'

'Well, what on earth am I supposed to do?' she ranted, finally losing her grip on her temper. 'Lick them clean?'

'At least it would be something useful to do with your tongue,' he shot back, and stalked out of the kitchen, the dog slinking anxiously at his heels.

Lucie thought she was going to scream. At the very least she was going to throw something! She stormed out of the door before she hurled a pan through the window, grabbed a pile of newspapers from the lobby—presumably he wouldn't mind her using them—and headed off in her car to retrieve his precious floor bricks.

How was she supposed to know they were so special? Darn the man, he didn't have to be quite so evil about it! Something useful to do with her tongue, indeed!

Will phoned Richard, his senior partner, and told him about his arms.

'Lord! Are you all right?' he asked, his voice full of concern. 'Let me come round—'

'Richard, I'm fine. I've got Lucie here, don't forget.'

'Lucie?'

'Compton—our new registrar?'

'Ah, yes. Lucie.' Something shifted in his voice. 'How is she? Dear girl.'

Will rolled his eyes. 'She's in fine form. She's a tyrant. My house isn't my own.'

'Excellent. I'm sure she's doing a grand job. Just don't alienate her—she can do your locum work until you recover. You can train her—you *are* still well enough to do that, aren't you?'

'Barely,' he admitted grudgingly. 'I can't write— I can't hold anything in my hand. I've got to go back to the hospital for a check-up and a cast—they've only put a back-slab on.'

'Want me to come and take you?'

He was tempted, but for some perverse reason he

wanted Lucie to do it. To torture him even more by exposure to her endless cheer and mindless chatter? Or was it something to do with the firm press of those taut little buttocks in her jeans, and the pert tilt of her breasts beneath that silky soft sweater?

He dragged his mind back into order. 'I'll be fine. I'll bribe Lucie with a take-away,' he told Richard, and went and watched her from the bedroom window.

He could see her in the distance, struggling with the bricks, hauling them out of the puddles and plopping them into the car. Hers, thankfully, not his. She was going to be furious, of course, and he could have been a bit kinder about it, but his arm hurt and he was frustrated by the pain and the disability.

She came back an hour later, muddy and dishevelled, and hosed the bricks off on the yard. She looked even madder than she had yesterday, and he lurked quietly out of the way, his conscience pricking. Then Amanda came down to ride her horse, and introduced herself to Lucie, and moments later was heading for the kitchen at a lope.

Damn. Lucie must have told her about his accident. Amanda had been fussing round him already, and would, no doubt, seize this opportunity to ingratiate herself with him. She knocked on the door and came in, her eyes anxiously scanning him for signs of damage.

'Are you all right? You poor love! Fancy falling off the ladder! Anything I can do for you?'

He shook his head. 'No, really, I'm fine. Lucie's looking after me.'

Something that could have been jealousy flashed in her eyes. 'There's no need for that—you don't want strangers doing those sorts of things for you. I could help—'

'No, really,' Will cut in quickly. The very thought of Amanda 'helping' him chilled his blood, and he didn't dare to hazard a guess at what 'those sorts of things' might be. He suppressed a shudder. 'I'll be fine. My left hand's good—see?' He held it up and waggled it, stifling a moan of pain, and grinned convincingly. He hoped.

'Oh. Well, OK, then, but if there's anything I can do, you will ask, won't you?'

'Of course—and thank you.'

She paused at the door. 'Is she staying in the cottage?'

A hellion in him rose to the surface of the scummy pond that was his integrity. 'Lucie?' he said innocently. 'Ah—no. She's staying here—with me.' He winked, just for good measure, and Amanda coloured and backed away.

'Um. Right. OK. Well, take care.'

He felt guilty. She was a nice enough girl, but she was so—well, wholesome, really. Earnest and energetic and frightfully jolly.

And he was a rat.

He sighed. He was thirsty, and the orange juice in the carton was finished. He contemplated the scissors, and got another carton out of the fridge, wincing and juggling it onto the cast to support the weight. He dropped it on the worktop, picked the scissors up in his left hand and proceeded to mash the corner of the carton, not very effectively.

Of course, a decent brand of orange juice would have a pull tab, but that would probably have been beyond him, too, he was philosophical enough to realise.

He managed to chew a small hole in it with the scissors, then squeezed it out over a glass. Typically, he ended up with juice soaking down inside the back-slab and drenching the Tubigrip on the other hand. There was damn all in the glass, of course.

Disgusted, he balanced the carton on his cast, tipped it to his mouth and drank it through the mangled hole.

And of course that was how Lucie found him moments later.

She cocked a brow at him, squeezed past and washed her hands and arms in the sink. 'Couldn't you wait?'

'No. I was thirsty. Want some?'

She gave him a withering look, took a glass out of the cupboard and filled it with water, then drained it in a couple of swallows. How did women manage to find their way around kitchens so damned fast?

'Do you want to drink that out of the carton leaking all over your shirt, or would you rather I put some in a glass for you?'

One day, he thought, his pride was going to choke him. He hesitated, then gave up. 'Would you mind?' he said meekly.

She shot him a suspicious look and relieved him of the carton, trimming the opening straight and pouring it neatly into a fresh glass. 'Don't you have to go for a check-up today?' she asked as he drank.

'Mmm.'

'So shouldn't we go?'

'Probably. I've got juice all over these, I could do with some fresh supports.'

'I'm sure they'll oblige.'

She helped him into his sweater, then led the way to her car. He eyed it in dismay.

'Your car? Really?'

She paused in the act of getting in, one hand on the roof, the other on the top of the door. 'Really,' she vowed, refusing to relent. Yesterday had been quite enough. 'You can move the seat back,' she conceded.

She leant across and opened the door, pushing it ajar for him. He folded himself into the seat with much grunting, and slid it back when she lifted the adjustment lever.

'Are you in?'

'Just about,' he muttered ungraciously, and she leant across him to pull the door shut.

Hard, muscled thighs tensed under her weight as she sprawled over him, and she regretted not getting out and going round to close it. She hoisted herself upright, conscious of the heat in her cheeks and the gimlet gaze of Amanda watching them from beside the barn, and fastened his seat belt.

'That woman's got the hots for you,' she said candidly, watching Amanda in the rear-view mirror as they pulled away and hoping Will didn't misconstrue her remark as jealousy.

Apparently not. He rolled his eyes and groaned. 'Tell me about it,' he muttered. 'I'm afraid I rather exaggerated our—er—relationship. She was offering to help me in all sorts of hideously personal ways, so I'm afraid I used you as a way out. No doubt she'll hate you.'

Lucie spluttered with laughter, and Will's lips twitched. Not a smile—quite—but almost.

Maybe working with him wouldn't be so bad after all...

'Right, you met Richard at your interview, and this is Kathy, and Simon's about somewhere, and then there are all the receptionists, the practice manager, the practice and community nurses, the midwives...'

Lucie smiled and nodded and hoped she could remember a tenth of what he was telling her.

It all made sense, of course, and in many ways it was just like her city-centre practice had been, but in other ways it couldn't have been more different.

Take the setting, for example. Her London practice had been in a converted Victorian house, with a rabbit warren of rooms and corridors and odd little corners. This was modern, purpose built and astonishingly unprovincial.

All the equipment and methods in both were right up to date, of course, as they had to be in a training practice, but of the two environments, she had to say this was lighter and more spacious. Whether that was better or not she wasn't sure yet.

She had a pang of nostalgia for the untidy pile of anomalies she'd left behind, and a moment of fear that it wouldn't work out. She would have stayed in the other practice, given a choice, but she hadn't been. The trainer had had a heart attack and had had to take early retirement, and that had left nobody in the practice to take over.

It was only by luck that this vacancy had come up when it had.

She just hoped it was *good* luck.

Will had finished the introductions, and they went into his consulting room and settled down to start her first surgery. 'I'm going to sit in for a few days, make sure you've got all the referrals and so on at your fingertips and that you're up to speed on the way we do things. Then, if we're both happy, I'll leave you to it,' he said.

Great. An audience. And she'd thought driving the car had been bad!

Her first patient was a girl of fifteen, whose mother had brought her in 'because there's nothing wrong with her and I want you to tell her so, Doctor.'

Lucie and Will exchanged glances, and Lucie smiled at the girl. 'Let's see, you're Clare, aren't you?'

'Yes.' She coughed convulsively, and Lucie frowned. She'd already noticed that the teenager had been short of breath when they'd come in, and, unlike her other practice, there were no stairs here to blame!

'Tell me what seems to be wrong,' she coaxed, but the mother butted in again.

'She should have gone back to school today, but she's been flopping about and coughing for the last week, and she's got exams coming up—she's doing her GCSEs and she can't afford to have time off!'

'So what's the matter, Clare?' Lucie asked again. 'Tell me in what way you aren't feeling quite right.'

'My cough,' she began.

'She's not eating. She's starving herself to death—I think she's got anorexia or something. I think the cough is just a big put-on, but if you give her antibiotics she won't have any excuse, she won't be able to swing the lead. I've given her a good talking-to about this eating business. Dr Ryan, you tell her.'

Will shook his head and smiled. 'Dr Compton is

quite capable of making a diagnosis, Mrs Reid. We'll let her see what she comes up with first, shall we?'

Lucie felt like a bug under a microscope. Will had thrown his support behind her, but almost in the form of a challenge, and now she had to find something wrong. She was just warming up to her 'we can't give out antibiotics like sweets' talk, when Clare coughed again.

Listen to her chest, her common sense advised, and, to her huge relief, there was a crackle. Her face broke into a broad smile. 'There's your answer— she's got a chest infection. No anorexia, no skiving, just a genuine sick girl who needs antibiotics.'

'Well, that was easy. I thought you didn't dish them out these days?' Mrs Reid said sceptically, looking to Will for reassurance.

'Only when necessary,' Lucie confirmed, 'and with all those crackles in her chest, trust me, it's necessary. It sounds like someone eating a packet of crisps in there.'

Clare giggled, clearly relieved to have been taken seriously, and Lucie smiled at her. 'You'll soon feel better. You need to rest, drink lots and get back to school as soon as you feel right. When do you do your exams, is it this year or next?'

'Next year, the real thing, but we've got end-of-year ones coming up after half-term, and Dad'll kill me if I don't do well.' She pulled a face. 'He's a teacher.'

Lucie laughed. 'I know the feeling. My father's a teacher, too. He used to look at me over his half-glasses and say, ''You don't seem to be doing very much homework these days.'' It drove me nuts— especially as I was working my socks off!'

'I bet he's pleased with you now, though,' Clare said thoughtfully. 'I want to be a doctor, too, but I don't know if I'm clever enough.'

'You know, there are lots of things you can do apart from medicine in the medical field. Wait and see how it pans out. Your grades might be good enough, and if not, there are lots of other options.'

Will cleared his throat quietly in the background, and Lucie looked at him. He was staring pointedly at the clock on the wall, and she gulped guiltily and brought up the girl's details on the computer, printed off her prescription and sent her and her over-anxious mother away.

Then she sat back and waited for the lecture.

He said nothing.

She looked at him. 'Aren't you going to criticise me?'

He smiled smugly and shook his head. 'Oh, yes—but later. I think your next patient has had to wait quite long enough, don't you?'

She stifled the urge to hit him.

CHAPTER THREE

IT WAS lunchtime. Apart from Clare, her first case, she had seen another fifteen patients that morning— and overrun surgery by an hour.

Now they were going on visits and, because she didn't know the way, Will was having to direct her.

Which meant, of course, that his mouth was busy with 'Turn left, go up there, it's on the right,' instead of 'Why didn't you do such and such?'. That was a huge relief to Lucie, who was coping—just—with his presence, without the added burden of her sins being heaped upon her head.

Actually she thought the surgery had gone quite well, but several times she'd caught Will rolling his eyes in the background or flicking glances at the clock. Had he been able to write, she knew he would have been making copious notes on her abysmal performance.

Tough. Anyway, it wasn't abysmal. Just a tad slow. She told herself it was because she was being thorough.

'Go along that road there to the end,' he instructed. 'It's the white house near the corner.'

There were two white houses near the corner. Of course she pulled up outside the wrong one, and couldn't resist the smirk of satisfaction when he objected.

He heaved a sigh, went to stab his hand through his hair and clonked his head with the cast.

'You should have a sling on,' she reminded him.

'I don't like slings. They mess my neck up.'

'Your hand will swell.'

'That's fine, there's room, it's still got the back-slab on.'

'Only because you won't wear a sling!'

Will turned to her, his eyes flying sparks. 'Lucie, it's my arm. If I don't want to wear a sling, I won't wear a sling. I most particularly won't wear two slings. And I won't be nagged by a junior doctor that I'm training!'

'I am not a junior doctor,' she bit out through clenched teeth. 'I am a registrar. I am not a complete incompetent, whatever you might think, and how you got the job of trainer I can't imagine. You're patronising, unfairly critical and judgmental.'

'I haven't said a word—'

'Yet! No doubt it's coming.'

He sat back and studied her curiously. 'So what did you think you did wrong this morning?' he asked with studied calm.

'Apart from breathe?' Lucie muttered under her breath. 'Overran the surgery time.'

'What else?'

'Nothing,' she said defensively.

'I would have got a sputum sample from Clare to make sure she'd got the right antibiotic.'

Oh, would he? Damn. He was right, and she would have done if he hadn't put her off by clearing his throat pointedly and looking at the clock. She wondered if Clare had taken the first dose yet, or if she should ring—

'I've rung and ordered it. They'll pick the pot up before she takes the first dose,' Will added, as if he'd read her mind. 'They live very close to the surgery. What else?'

She stuffed her irritation into a mental pending tray to deal with later and scanned through her morning list. 'That man with indigestion-like pain—'

'Mr Gregory.'

'Yes. He's obese.'

'Actually, technically he's just overweight. His body mass index is 29.4. He's working on getting it down, but he's aiming for a 10 kg weight loss. That's probably why he's got indigestion. Faddy diets and varied eating habits can cause that.'

'It would have been helpful to know that before the consultation. I was wondering about the choice between angina and *Helicobacter pylori*, and it's probably just too much cucumber!'

A flicker of guilt came and went in his eyes. 'Sorry. It's the painkillers. I'm not really concentrating. You're right.'

Lucie's jaw nearly dropped. An apology? Good grief, wonders will never cease, she thought.

'Since you're on a roll, I don't suppose you want to apologise for that remark about licking the bricks, do you?' she challenged, pushing her luck.

He smiled. It was a dangerous, predatory smile. 'Not really,' he said, and opened the car door with a wince. 'Let's get on or we'll be late.'

'So, are you going to tell me about this patient, or let me go in blind?' she asked his retreating form.

He sat back, letting the door fall shut and looking at her over his shoulder. 'He's fifty-five or so, he's had a heart attack, he's been under a cardiologist but cancelled his follow-up appointment on a flimsy pretext. I reckon he's in line for bypass surgery but he

won't stick to a diet or exercise programme and he
keeps getting chest pain. This is just a routine check-
up. I suggest you take routine obs while I talk.'

'I thought I was taking on your patients?' she objected, but he shook his head.

'Not this one. His wife's too nice—she doesn't
deserve all this worry. She needs moral support.'

'And I can't give it?'

'Not like I can. I've known her for years,' he
pointed out fairly.

'Not that many, Old Father Time. How old are
you?'

He shot her a grin. 'I've been here six years.
We've gone through the menopause together, Pam
and I. I know her well, trust me.'

She gave a quiet and not very ladylike snort as he
got out of the car. Retrieving her bag from the back,
she locked the car and followed him across the road.

A woman was standing in the front garden of the
other white house, stripping off bright yellow rubber
gloves, and he bent and kissed her cheek. 'Hello,
Pam,' he said gently. 'How are things?'

She rolled her eyes despairingly, then shot him a
keen look. 'Never mind me—is that a cast on your
arm? *And* a bandage on the other one—what on earth
have you been up to?'

He told her the story, played down the drama and
played up the farce, and introduced Lucie as the cav-
alry. 'Very timely arrival, although, of course, if she
hadn't been coming I wouldn't have been mending
the roof of the cottage and I wouldn't have been up
the ladder, so in a way it's her fault.'

'That's right, blame me,' Lucie said, rolling her

eyes and laughing. 'Although as I remember it, you were rescuing the cat, actually.'

'She's doing all the physical stuff for me, I'm doing the talking,' Will explained, cutting her off with a grin. 'She's our new trainee registrar.'

'Are you? Poor you,' Pam said comfortingly. 'He can be a bit of a slave-driver, I gather. His last one left in a hurry.'

'His last one was useless,' Will pointed out fast. 'Don't slag me off, Pam, she already thinks I've got a broomstick stashed in the barn.'

'Yes—a Swedish one,' Lucie chipped in. 'Estate version.'

He laughed, not unkindly. 'It's a lovely car.'

'It's too big.'

'We're using it tomorrow. That thing of yours gives me backache and cramp.'

'Poor baby.'

Pam eyed them with curiosity. 'I think you'll survive, Lucie,' she said consideringly, and smiled at her. 'Welcome to Bredford.'

'Thank you.' She returned the smile, comforted that at least someone was going to be on her side, and followed them in.

Their patient was sitting in an upright chair, a folded newspaper on the floor at his side and a cup of what looked like very strong coffee on the table next to him.

'Hello, Dick,' Will said easily, perching on the sofa near their patient's chair. 'I won't shake hands, I've mashed myself. This is Lucie Compton, my new registrar.'

Lucie shook hands with him, noticing the pallor of his skin except for the high flush over his nose and cheekbones, and wondered just how bad his heart condition was.

'Lucie, why don't you run the ruler over him while we chat, to save time?' Will suggested, and she opened her bag and took out her stethoscope, listening to the patient's chest first to hear his heart.

It was a little irregular, but without an ECG it was difficult to tell what was wrong about it. His chest was clear, at least. She took his pulse and respiration, while Will propped his arms on his knees and smiled at Dick encouragingly. 'So, tell me, how are you doing?'

'Oh, not so bad.'

'He's been getting chest pain.'

Will looked from Dick to Pam and back again. 'On exertion, or at rest?'

'At night. At least, that's when I know about it,' Pam confirmed.

Will nodded. 'And how about the daytime, Dick? Anything then?'

The man shrugged. 'Off and on.'

'Are you taking the pills?'

'Yes.'

'No.'

Will's eyes flicked to Pam again. 'He's not?'

She shook her head. 'Not always. Not unless I nag him.'

'Which she does all the time, of course,' Dick put in with a rueful, indulgent smile. 'Oh, I don't know, Will, I just feel there's no point. I'm a great believer in Fate. If my number's up, it's up. I'm not going to bugger up the rest of my life taking pills and watching what I eat and drink. It's like the old joke about giving up drinking, women and red meat. It doesn't make you live longer, it just feels that way!'

Will chuckled obediently, and glanced at Pam again. 'I wouldn't suggest you give up women—at least, not this one. She's a star. But the food and drink are real issues, Dick. The next step down the line for you could be bypass surgery, and you really owe it to yourself to be as fit as possible for it.'

'Oh, I know. You're going to tell me to lay off the booze, cut my fat intake and get off my backside and walk two miles a day, aren't you?'

'Something like that. Sounds as if you've heard it before somewhere. And while we're at it, I'll throw in caffeine. Decaff tea and coffee, please.'

Lucie bent down to her bag to remove the blood-pressure cuff, and hid a smile. Dick curled his lip. 'Decaff? Filthy stuff.'

'Rubbish. You can't tell the difference.'

'I can.'

'So drink fruit teas or orange juice.'

Will was treated to another withering look. 'Fruit teas,' Dick said disgustedly.

'Unlaced.'

He shook his head slowly. 'You're a hard man.'

'I'm trying to keep you alive. No point in dying on the waiting list, Dick—always assuming you ever get on it. Have you made another appointment yet?'

Something flickered in Dick's eyes—something that could have been fear.

'Not yet. Keep forgetting.'

Lucie slipped the blood-pressure cuff off his arm and chipped in.

'A patient at my last practice had a by-pass op. He felt like you—what was the point? If it was going to get him, there was no point in worrying. He felt so much better after the op, he realised it had been worth worrying about. I had a letter from him the other day. He's taken early retirement, moved to the country and started playing golf, and he feels great. He's lost two stone, he's fitter than he's been for years and he says there's a twinkle in his wife's eye that's been missing for ages.'

Dick moistened his lips and cleared his throat. 'He feels better?'

'Yes. He felt better straight away. His chest was a bit sore for a while, of course, but he said the hospital were excellent and it was more than worth it. He sent me a photo—he looks terrific. Why don't you give it the benefit of the doubt and find out more?'

He looked thoughtful, and Lucie put the rest of her equipment away and straightened up. 'That all seems OK,' she said to Will. 'Anything else you want me to check?'

He shook his head and stood up. 'Listen to us, Dick. We aren't all telling you the same thing by coincidence, you know. Give it a whirl.'

Dick nodded grudgingly, and Will looked at Pam. 'Your garden's looking good. You must show me round it on the way out—I want to see your osteo-spermums. I can't believe you overwinter them out-side. Mine all die without fail.'

Gardening already, for heaven's sake! Lucie cleared her throat, and glanced pointedly at her watch. Will ignored her.

'I've got some cuttings I've done for you—come down to the greenhouse and I'll give them to you,' Pam was saying.

'You're a marvel.'

Lucie sighed. 'I'll wait here,' she said, and sat down again with Dick. Maybe she could spend the time usefully after all...

For a moment he didn't speak, then he looked at her searchingly. 'Now tell me the truth. How much will it hurt after the op?'

Right for the jugular. 'A lot,' she said honestly, 'but less than another heart attack. The breastbone is the worst bit, and the leg can be quite sore for a few days, apparently, but they give you pain relief intravenously, and you have control over that. If it hurts, you can give yourself a shot, and it really does make it bearable. Everyone who's had it says it's worth it.'

He nodded, and licked his lips nervously. 'I'm scared,' he confessed. 'I can't tell Pam—seems so silly, really, to be afraid of pain, but I've never been good with it. Pam wants me to have it done privately to cut the waiting time, but I don't want to, even though we've got private health insurance as part of my work package. I suppose there's a bit of me that would rather wait longer and maybe die, so I don't have to deal with it. Does that seem strange to you?'

Lucie shook her head and smiled. 'No. Quite normal. Most people aren't afraid of being dead. They're afraid of suffering. I think you're actually very ordinary like that. Nobody likes pain. The thing is, if you have another heart attack, there's no guarantee it will kill you, but it will make you less well for the operation and it will, of course, be very painful in itself. I think at the very least you should see a cardiologist and discuss it.'

'I just—it scares me.'

'I take it you've had an angiogram and aren't suitable for balloon angioplasty?' she said as an after-thought.

He shook his head. 'No. They were talking about it, but I didn't know what it was.'

'So ask.'

'Everyone's always busy.'

Lucie smiled. 'That's life for you. An angiogram is a diagnostic image of the heart with radio-opaque dye injected into the coronary arteries, so they can see just where the arteries are clogging.'

'Oh, I had that. I never got the results, though. I thought you meant the other thing. The pasty thing.'

'Plasty. Angioplasty. If you're a suitable candidate, there's always the possibility that you won't have to have bypass surgery. Lots of people have balloon angioplasty instead. That's where they stick a little inflatable catheter in through a nick in the groin, track it with X-rays until it's in the right place and inflate it. It stretches the arteries and relieves the narrow point, if it's just one small constriction. And, of course, until you get the results of the angiogram, you won't know.'

Dick nodded. 'You're right, of course. I'll go back. I will. Thanks.'

'My pleasure. Have you got a computer? If you have, you could find out more about it on the inter-net. It's brilliant for things like that.' Lucie stood up. 'You will keep the appointment this time, won't you? It can't hurt to find out, and even if you ended up with surgery, you could have a whole new life ahead of you. Think of all the years you've worked, just to throw it all away before you retire.' She glanced at her watch again. 'I must go—we've got lots of other visits to do yet and I'm already running behind. It's only my first day.'

'And Will with broken arms, eh? Still, he's got such a nice, even temper. Anyone else might be really grumpy.'

Lucie nearly choked, swallowing the retort. Instead she smiled at Dick, exorted him to give the consultant a chance and reached the door just as Will and Pam came in.

'Right, are you all done?' Will asked. He had plant pots balanced on his cast, and Lucie rolled her eyes.

'Scrounging off the patients?' she teased as they went out to the car.

'Absolutely. Cheers, Pam. Thanks. Cheerio, Dick. Mind how you go.'

Lucie stuck her keys in the door of the car and paused. 'It would never happen in the city,' she remarked over the roof in a quiet voice.

'It's a cover. She wanted to talk to me about him. He won't go back to the consultant.'

'Yes, he will,' Lucie said smugly. 'I just talked him into it—at least, I think I did. The only reason he wouldn't do it is because he's afraid of the pain. He's hoping he'll die before he gets to the front of the waiting list. I told him it was possible he'd be suitable for balloon angioplasty, and even if he wasn't, how about his retirement?'

Will stared at her over the top of the car. 'And you've talked him round?'

'Yup.'

Respect dawned in his eyes. 'Good girl, well done,' he said softly. 'It's a shame he can't afford to go privately and get it over with, now he's psyched up. Not that it should be necessary, but I don't want to start on the politics of funding.'

'Pointless, really,' Lucie said with a cheeky grin. 'We'd probably be in agreement, and that would never do, would it? Anyway, he's got private health insurance through his work.'

She opened the car, slid behind the wheel and pushed his door open. He tried to pass the plants to her, but, of course, he dropped one on the seat, and it splattered wet black compost all over her upholstery.

'''Don't you dare put those bricks in my car like that,''' she mimicked, and he groaned and met her eyes, his own apologetic.

'I'm sorry.'

'Don't fret, I don't have to sit on it. Just brush it off for now—you can lick it clean later.'

Shooting her a foul look, he used his sprained wrist to flick the little bits of black aside, leaving dirty streaks on his bandage and the seat.

She stifled a smile. 'On second thoughts, using your car in future might be a good idea, if you're going to take up horticulture as a sideline,' she said sweetly. 'Mind you don't stand on them.'

He clenched his jaw and got into the car, tucking his arm into the seat belt and pulling it through with care and much wincing. She let him struggle for a moment, then took the buckle and clipped it in.

Her hand brushed his thigh, and it tensed again as it had before. She stifled another smile. Interesting.

'When are you going to go back to the hospital? You ought to go to the fracture clinic.'

'I'll go tomorrow,' he said. 'Right, where to next?'

* * *

Lucie was right, of course, he did need a sling on it, but now his pride was going to get in the way and so he surreptitiously propped his right arm up on anything that was handy, just to take the pressure off it.

It was pounding and, of course, with only a back-slab it was marginally unstable, too, and grated nicely every now and again if he was a bit rash. He really should get it seen to, he thought with a sigh.

The day seemed to drag interminably, and Lucie didn't need to be watched every second. She was more than capable of running his afternoon clinic on her own, and in the end he left her to it and called a patient who ran a minicab.

He was an ex-London cabbie, and always good value, and he entertained Will all the way to the hospital. He took himself off for a cup of tea while Will saw the fracture clinic staff and got a lecture about the swelling and resting it in a sling. Then the cabbie took him home, after Will had bribed the man to go down his track.

'Blimey, gov, it's a miracle nobody's got stuck on this,' he said in a broad Cockney accent.

'Mmm,' Will agreed noncommitally, saying nothing about Lucie. He gave the man a hefty tip, crawled into the house and greeted Bruno with guarded enthusiasm.

'Hello, mate. Good dog, get off. Ouch!' He raised his arms out of reach, kneed the dog out of the way and sat down at the table with his arms in front of him, safe. Now all he needed was some pills, and they, of course, were in his pocket. Could he get them out?

He struggled, but came up with them, and even

managed to open the lid. Amazing. He took two, thought about another and put the lid back on. He'd have more later. In the meantime, he was going to stretch out on the sofa with the dog at his feet and have forty winks…

'Hello, Lucie. How are you doing?'

She looked up from her paperwork and smiled at Richard Brayne, the senior partner. 'Oh, hi, there. I'm fine. I don't know where Will is—have you seen him?'

'Gone to the fracture clinic and then home, he said.' Richard settled himself beside her and pushed a mug of tea across the table to her. 'You must be doing well if he'll leave you alone all ready.'

'Or he feels like death warmed up, which is more likely,' Lucie said drily, harbouring no illusions about her brilliance or Will's understanding of it. 'I suppose he wants me to cover his evening surgery— is he on call tonight, by any chance, just to add to the joys?'

Richard shook his head and grinned. 'No. You get lucky. We have night cover—a co-operative. You don't have to do any nights. Will doesn't—he has too much to do on the farm.'

Lucie tipped her head and looked searchingly at Richard, puzzled. 'On the farm?' she asked. 'Such as what?'

'Oh, I don't know, fencing the fields, mending the barn, doing up the house, getting the cottage ready for guests. He's always busy. Just at the moment he's redoing the ground floor of the house, I think—or he was.'

Lucie was relieved. She had wondered, for a mo-

ment there, if he had masses of stock all starving to
death without him—stock she was about to have to
look after. She didn't mind the dog or the cat, and
she'd get used to the snorting horse given time, but
anything more agricultural was beyond her.

It was a pity, she thought on her way back there
later that evening, that Will didn't spend some of that
time being busy doing the drive. She picked her way
along it with caution, and went in to find him
sprawled full length on the sofa.

Bruno had greeted her rapturously, whining and
wagging and pushing his great face into her hand,
and she'd patted him and done the 'good dog' thing,
and had then looked for Will.

And there he was, spark out, looking curiously
vulnerable this time. There was a sling round his
neck but the arm was out of it, propped beside him
on a pillow with a cool pack over the gap in the back
of the plaster. He'd obviously been ticked off at the
fracture clinic, she thought with wry amusement, and
was now doing as he was told.

Or perhaps the pain had finally penetrated his common sense. Whatever, he was now doing what he
should have been doing ever since he'd hurt himself.

Finally, she thought, and then wondered what was
for supper.

Whatever she cooked, she realised. She went into
the kitchen, followed by the clearly hopeful dog, and
fed him first. The cat materialised at the sound of
Bruno's bowl clunking round the floor, and she fed
her, too.

'OK, guys, what about us?' she asked, and Bruno
cocked his head on one side for a moment, before
going back to his optimistic licking.

She found some steak mince in the freezer, and onions and tinned tomatoes and some ready-made Bolognese sauce, and in the cupboard next to the sink, under the first-aid kit, she found a bag of pasta shells.

Easy—and he could eat it without difficulty. She threw it together, dished up and went and woke him.

'Supper's ready,' she announced, and he propped himself up groggily on his left elbow and peered at her out of dazed eyes.

'Supper?'

'Spag Bol. Well, pasta shells, anyway.'

'Oh, God.' He pulled a face and flopped back down on the cushions. 'Right at the moment, I can't think of anything I want less.'

She stared at him in amazement, then flipped. 'Fine,' she said tightly. 'I'm sure it'll find a more appreciative audience.'

And she stalked into the kitchen, seized his plate and scraped it into the dog's bowl, just as Will came through the doorway.

'What the hell are you doing?' he asked, stunned.

She banged the bowl down defiantly. 'You said you didn't want it.'

'No, I said I couldn't think of anything I wanted less than food. That didn't mean I wouldn't have eaten it! Hells teeth, woman!'

He stared with evident dismay at the dog, who had swallowed the plateful almost whole and was busy doing the dish-licking thing again.

Throwing her one last disbelieving look, he let his breath out on a sharp sigh, turned on his heel and went back into the sitting room, banging the door behind him.

Whoops. OK. So she'd overreacted. Hardly the first time, but he just seemed to set her off. She looked at her own food with regret. She could give it to him...

Or she could eat it, and he could contemplate the wisdom of thinking before he spoke. She was sure he managed it with his patients, so why not her?

No. She was eating it. All of it. Every bite.

It nearly choked her.

Will was starving. Only pride prevented him from going into the kitchen and making himself something to eat—pride and the fact that Lucie was in there with the radio on, singing along to some ghastly noise and chattering to the dog, who was her devoted slave.

'Fickle beast,' he mumbled, flicking through the television channels with the remote control in his reluctant left hand. He found a wildlife programme, and settled down to watch it, disturbed only by the noise from the kitchen.

After five minutes, it had driven him crazy. He stood up, walked over to the door and yanked it open, just stifling the little yelp of pain in time. 'Do you suppose you could turn that bloody awful racket down?' he snarled, and kicked the door shut again, retreating to the sofa to nurse his throbbing wrist.

'Sor-ry,' she carolled through the door, and then started humming and singing, which was worse, because she had a throaty, sexy voice that did unforgivable things to his libido.

He turned the TV up in self-defence, and forced himself to concentrate on the mating habits of some obscure Australian spider. Riveting it wasn't, and fi-

nally he went upstairs to bed, propped himself up
and read a book until he'd heard Lucie settle for the
night.

Then, like a fugitive in his own home, he crept
down to the kitchen, raided the bread bin and managed painfully and raggedly to hack the end off the
loaf.

He found a chunk of cheese in the fridge, looked
in despair at the tub of olive-oil spread and realised
that the effort was more than he could be bothered
to make. He wrapped the cheese in the wavering
doorstep of dry bread, bit the end off and poured a
glass of milk. It would have to do. Anything else
was beyond him.

He carried the rustic little snack up to bed, wondering as he went where Bruno was, and then saw
him through the crack in Lucie's door, curled up
across the foot of her bed, one eye open and tail
waving gently in apology at his defection.

Lucie was scrunched up at the top, forced out by
the dog, and he smiled nastily. Good. Serve her right.
If there was any justice Bruno would be sick on her
floor and she'd have to clear it up—and lying like
that she'd almost inevitably wake up with a crick in
her neck.

He sighed and shook his head. Lord, she really
brought out the worst in him, but she was so disrup-
tive! He was used to silence, broken only by the
sounds of nature or by the television or radio if he
chose to have them on, which he often didn't.

It wasn't her fault she was here, of course. The
sooner he got the bed ordered, the sooner he could
have his peace and quiet back. He vowed to do it the
next day.

First thing in the morning...

CHAPTER FOUR

'WHAT do you mean, you can't do it till next week?'

'Sorry, sir, all our carpet-fitters are busy. It's because of the spring, you see.'

Will didn't. All he saw was the next week stretching ahead of him, fighting with Lucie for his personal space.

'But surely you can manage one small room.'

'That's what they all say, sir,' the salesman told him cheerfully. 'Next Wednesday's the earliest we can possibly get to you.'

'But I have to have it!' He heard the rising, frenzied tone and cleared his throat, dropping his voice an octave and striving for authority. 'I really have to have it,' he insisted, and then added coaxingly, 'Can't you manage this Friday? Perhaps for an incentive payment?'

'Not even if you double it, sir,' the man said implacably. 'If you really are in such a hurry, I suggest you buy a piece off the roll and fit it yourself.'

'I might just do that,' he lied. 'Elsewhere.' If he had arms. Hah. He would have hung up with a flourish, but remembered just in time that it would hurt too much. Instead, he replaced the receiver with exaggerated care and swore, just as Lucie came back into the consulting room bearing two cups of coffee and a pile of patient envelopes.

'No joy?' she said sweetly, plonking the mug down in front of him, and if he'd had two hands, he would have strangled her while she was in range. Instead, he withdrew into dignity.

'There are other firms,' he said tautly. 'I shall keep trying. Are those this morning's notes?'

'No, tomorrow's. I thought we could get ahead.'

'Don't get sarky,' he growled, and her lips twitched. Aggravating woman. He dragged his eyes off her lips and tried to stop fantasising about them. He had to concentrate...

Will seemed to be getting a little better, Lucie thought as the day wore on, if his temper was anything to go by. He was crabbier than ever, possibly from pain, but more likely because now he was over the initial shock of his fall, the enforced inactivity was starting to get to him. By all accounts he was usually a busy person, and just now he was having to put up and shut up. It clearly didn't sit well on him.

Nor did not being able to drive, and her refusal to drive his car instead of hers. 'I hate it,' she'd insisted. 'We take mine or we don't go—or you can pay for a taxi.'

It hadn't really been fair, and in truth there was nothing at all wrong with the bigger car. It was easy to drive, but she was used to hers, and anyway, it was the principle.

So he'd folded himself up and threaded himself through the door like a camel through the eye of the needle, and sat in grim-lipped silence most of the time they were out.

And then, after their last call, he climbed out of the car and winced, and she noticed he was limping.

Oh, blast. Guilt washed over her, and she hurried after him.

'Are you OK?' she asked with genuine concern, and he shot her a look like a shard of ice.

'Just peachy. How the hell do you think I am?'

She shrugged. 'Just asking.'

'Well, don't bother,' he snapped. 'Everything hurts like the devil.'

'Did you take your painkillers earlier?' she asked, and got another murderous look for her pains.

No, then. She made him a drink, and they talked through her calls until it was time for her afternoon clinic, and then, because it was a shared antenatal with the midwife and she had plenty of supervision, he took himself off to an empty consulting room.

'To sort this darned carpet out,' he said with determination, and she pitied the salesmen he was about to browbeat into submission.

She enjoyed the antenatal clinic. She'd always liked maternity, mainly because it was the one branch of medicine where everyone, by and large, was well. She felt her first set of triplets, and listened to their heartbeats, and discussed the management of the delivery with the midwife and the mother, Angela Brown.

It had been planned that she would have a hospital delivery by Caesarean section, and was being seen alternately at the hospital and the GP clinic. As the time went on, she would transfer entirely to the hospital, and although she was happy to do that for the sake of the babies, she expressed regret that it couldn't be a more normal birth.

'Are you looking forward to it?' Lucie asked,

wondering how she'd cope with three at once. Apparently she wasn't the only one wondering.

'Actually, I'm dreading it,' the patient confessed. 'I don't know how I'll manage. My mother's said she'll help, and my husband's going to take some time off, but it's going to be hell at first, and we're only in a small house. This wasn't exactly planned, and I was going back to work afterwards, but there's no way I can afford to pay child care for three!'

Good grief, Lucie thought. Accidental triplets on a tight budget? Rather her than me.

They finished their clinic, and she found Will in the office, hunched over a cup of tea. He looked up at her as she approached, and his lip moved a fraction. A smile? Perhaps his face muscles were on a tight budget, like Mrs Brown, she thought, and stifled a chuckle.

'Got your carpet sorted?' she asked, and a frown replaced the sorry excuse for a smile.

'More or less. I've had to pay more, but it comes on Monday. I thought it was worth it.'

She ignored the implied insult. 'So we'll be stuck with each other over the weekend,' she said breezily. 'I dare say we'll survive.'

He muttered something inaudible, and she felt another flicker of irritation and hurt. How silly of her. It wasn't personal, he just liked his space, she told herself. 'How about the bed?'

'From the same place. It'll come later in the day. I've arranged to leave them a key. Security's not a problem—nobody ever goes down my track except for the occasional dog walker who's got mislaid on the footpath from the ferry.'

She settled her chin on her hands and looked

across the table at him, wishing he wasn't quite so prickly with her. 'Tell me about this ferry,' she said, trying to bridge the gulf between them. 'When does it run? I've looked and looked, but I can't see anything.'

'You won't. It doesn't exist. It's just the name of the little jut of land. It used to be a chain ferry that crossed the mouth of the river, but they built a bridge further up. The only thing left is the name.'

'Oh.' And that was the end of that attempt at conversation. She switched to Mrs Brown and her triplets. 'I saw your triplet lady,' she told him. 'She's worried about how she'll cope.'

'She needs to,' he told her bluntly. 'Her husband's quite demanding, and I can't see him tolerating slipping standards. He didn't want her to have one—pressed for a termination before they even discovered it was three.'

Lucie was shocked. 'She didn't tell me that,' she murmured slowly. 'How sad. I wonder if they'll survive?'

'The triplets, or the Browns?'

'I meant the Browns, but all of them, really. The babies seem quite small.'

'Triplets often are, especially at term, and who knows what'll happen to them all? In their financial situation three babies is the last thing they need. Sometimes I'm glad I'm a GP, not a social worker.' He leant back, easing the kinks out of his shoulders and wincing. 'Right, what's next? No surgery tonight—no more calls to make. Do you have paperwork to deal with, or can we go?'

She blinked. 'No surgery?'

'Nope. Not on Tuesdays. Not for me, anyway.'

'Oh. Well, we can go, then. I'm all up to date. How about you? Are you supposed to go back to the fracture clinic?'

He held up his arm, and for the first time she saw the brand-new lightweight cast. 'Oh! You've been!'

'Ten out of ten,' he drawled sarcastically. 'Took you long enough to notice. I went while you were doing the antenatals.'

'That was very quick.'

'I charmed the plaster nurse,' he said, deadpan, and she wondered how on earth he'd done that. There was precious little sign of his charm being exercised around her. She pushed back her chair and stood up.

'Shall we go, then?'

'Sounds like a fine idea.'

He winced again as he threaded himself back into the car, and hit his head on the doorframe as he sat down. She ignored the muttered oath, and let him struggle with the seat belt for a moment before helping him with the clip.

'You really are rather big for this car, aren't you?' she conceded.

'Oh, the penny's dropped,' he said with thinly veiled sarcasm. 'Of course, a less obstructive person…'

He let the rest of the sentence hang, and she snapped her mouth shut and declined to comment. She was damned if she was going to tell him *now* that she'd decided to take his car in future. Let him stew on it for the night.

Talking of which…

'Should we call into a supermarket on the way and pick up some food? There's not a lot in your fridge.'

'Good idea. We can buy some ready meals so you don't have to cook.'

She shot him a sideways glance. Was that guilt after his reaction to her spaghetti dish last night, or a dig at her choice of menu? Whatever, if he chose the food, he couldn't complain that it was the last thing he wanted.

Besides, she didn't like cooking anyway—not your everyday meat and two veg stuff. She liked tinkering about with fancy ingredients and playing with dinner party menus, but that was all. Anything else was just basic nutrition to keep body and soul together, and it bored her senseless. She didn't normally succumb, but she had to admit that just for today an instant meal sounded fine.

Convenience foods, Will decided, were not all they were cracked up to be. He pushed the soggy pasta twirls round in the over-seasoned sauce and sighed. It didn't smell anything like as good as the Bolognese she'd made last night—the Bolognese she'd fed to the dog.

Still, Bruno didn't complain when he put the cardboard dish on the floor and let the dog finish it. Twice running, Will thought. The dog would be huge.

'Don't you like it?' Lucie asked, and his stomach growled.

'I'm not really hungry,' he lied. 'I'll make myself something later.'

She gave him a searching look. 'Do you want me to make you something? A bacon sandwich?'

His stomach growled even more enthusiastically, and he gave a wry, bitter little smile. 'Why would you do that?'

She stood up, dumped her plate on the floor in front of the bemused but receptive dog and headed for the fridge. 'Because I want one and it would seem churlish not to make yours? Because I don't like instant food any more than I imagine you do? Because I need you alive if I'm to finish my training? Take your pick.'

How about, Because I'm sorry I gave your dinner to the dog? Will wanted to suggest, but he thought he'd quit while he was winning. 'A bacon sandwich sounds fine,' he muttered, and then sighed inwardly. Did that sound a bit grudging? Oh, hell. He wasn't used to being dependent, and he didn't like it. 'Please,' he added, too late to be spontaneous, and caught her stifled smile out of the corner of his eye.

'While you do that I think I'll go and change,' he said, and went upstairs and struggled one-handed out of the trousers he'd been wearing for work. They had a hook fastening that was possible even with his reluctant arms, and a little easy-running nylon zip, but the belt was more of a problem. He shut the end in the door, tugged gently until the buckle was free and then slid the end out.

He was getting resourceful, he thought as he squirmed and shuffled his way into his jogging bottoms. Learning to adapt. One thing that was almost impossible, though, was washing. He'd managed so far—more or less—by removing the support on his left wrist and using his left hand, but it wasn't satisfactory and it hurt like hell. And it relied on Lucie to put the support back on.

He thought of the bath longingly. What he wanted more than anything in the world was a long, hot soak, but he didn't think he could manage without help, and he was damned if he was asking Lucie Compton to supervise his ablutions!

Perhaps he should ask Amanda, he thought with a wry twist of humour, and shuddered. The thought was terrifying. She'd probably rub him down with a dandy brush, to get his circulation going.

A wonderful smell of frying bacon drifted up the stairs, and he arrived back in the kitchen just as she set two plates down on the table. 'There you are,' she said cheerfully. 'Wrap yourself around that.'

He did, wondering idly where his five portions of fruit and veg were coming from that day, but there was no point in worrying. He'd eat an apple later. He'd rather have an orange, but he couldn't work out how to peel it.

'Um—about washing,' Lucie said, and he nodded his head towards the washing machine.

'Help yourself. Powder's in the cupboard.'

'Not clothes—you,' she corrected, and he felt a skittering moment of panic and anticipation.

'Me?' Will croaked, almost choking on a bite of sandwich.

'Well, you must be in need of a good long soak, I would have thought. Do you want me to wrap your cast up in plastic bags and run you a bath?'

Was she a mind-reader, or did he smell worse than he realised?

He sniffed experimentally. 'Is it that bad?' he asked, groping for a light note and managing instead to sound defensive.

Lucie gave a pitying smile. 'I just thought, by now, you must be feeling pretty dreadful. Of course,' she added lightly, 'there's always Amanda—perhaps you'd like me to give her a call and ask her to come over? I'm sure she'd be more than willing...'

'That won't be necessary,' he growled, not quite knowing how to take her teasing. 'I think I can manage—and before you offer, I don't need my back washed.'

Her lips twitched. 'I'm sure I'll live. Still, you can always yell if you get stuck. I don't suppose you've got anything that everybody else hasn't got.'

Except a body that even in adversity seemed hell bent on betraying his baser feelings! He focused on his sandwich. 'Thanks. Maybe later,' he said, knowing full well that he was going to take her up on it. He just hoped he didn't get stuck, because the consequences didn't bear thinking about!

Lucie's imagination was running riot. He'd been ages, and she was hovering in her bedroom, listening to every splash and groan. The door wasn't locked, of course. Not even Will Ryan was that bent on self-destruction.

'Are you OK?' she called.

'Fine,' he yelled, then added a belated, 'thanks.'

She shook her head and smiled. He really, really hated this. He was so stubborn and fiercely proud, and it was all so unnecessary. She was quite happy to help—if he only could bring himself to be at least civil about it!

While she waited, she thought it might be interesting to have a look at the rest of the house. So far she'd only seen the rooms they were using, and there were some intriguing doors...

'Can I look round the house?' she asked, pausing outside the bathroom, and there was a splash and a stream of something not quite audible. She decided she should be probably grateful for that.

'Sure,' he said shortly. 'Be careful upstairs, there's no light. There's a torch just inside the door. Mind the holes.'

Holes? Her curiosity well aroused, she opened the door and went through, flicking on the torch. Its powerful beam pierced the gloom, slicing through the dusty air and highlighting the cobwebs. She suppressed a shudder and looked around. It was all but derelict, or it had been. The roof was obviously repaired now—she could see that through the gaps where the ceiling had fallen down.

Beneath the holes in the ceiling were areas of rotten boards, some taken up, others just gaping and twisted. Some showed evidence of recent repair, to her comfort. She looked at the untouched parts, and rolled her eyes.

'Mind the holes' didn't even begin to scratch the surface! It was on a par with 'a bit rough in places', and typical of Will's under-estimation of the awfulness of a situation. She had visions of him telling a dying patient he'd feel 'a little bit dicky for a day or two'.

Mind the holes, indeed. She picked her way carefully down the long room, sticking to the patched bits, and peered out of the windows towards the distant river, eerily silvered with moonlight.

It would be a beautiful view in daylight, and the windows were positioned to take full advantage. She could see it would be a lovely room once it was repaired. Rooms, in fact. It would easily make two.

She glanced round again. No wonder he was frustrated with inactivity, if this was waiting for him! She

wondered if he'd done the work himself in the rest
of the house, or if he'd had the builders in.

Poor builders, she thought pityingly, and went
downstairs. Beyond the hall was the room below the
one she'd just investigated, and she opened the door
cautiously.

It was a mess. Well, to be exact it was a paint and
tool and timber store, and was obviously where he
kept everything for the work in progress. Again, it
was a lovely room, with a huge inglenook fireplace
on one wall and windows on three sides, and at least
this one had a light that worked, after a fashion—if
you counted a dangling bulb on the end of a bit of
flex.

It was heavily timbered, and there was a smell of
preservative in the air when she sniffed. Preservative
and mice. Lovely.

She shuddered and backed quickly out, bumping
into the dog and making herself jump.

'You scared me half to death, you stupid mutt!'
she told him with a nervous laugh, conveniently ignoring the fact that it had been her fault in the first
place. Conscious of the time, she went back upstairs
and listened at the bathroom door, Bruno at her heels.

She could hear nothing. She knocked lightly.
'Will? Are you OK?'

Absolute silence.

'Will?'

Oh, lord, what if he'd slipped and drowned while
she'd been downstairs out of earshot? She called his
name again, then, when he still didn't reply, she
pressed the lever down and inched the door open,
her heart in her mouth.

Please, God, don't let him be dead, she prayed

silently, and, pushing the door open, she took a step in.

He was asleep, his plastic-wrapped arm propped up on the side of the bath, his head lolling back against the end of the tub, his lashes dark against his pale cheeks. He was out for the count. Unable to help herself, she let her eyes wander over him—purely professionally, of course, to see how his bruises were progressing.

The water was soapy, but not that soapy. Not so cloudy that she couldn't see every inch of his beautifully made body. Where his chest and knees protruded from the water, wiry curls clung enticingly to the damp, sleek skin, emphasising his maleness.

Not that it needed emphasising, not with the water as clear as it was and none too deep, either. Oh, lord.

She backed away, retreating to safety, and took a long, steadying breath before rapping sharply on the door. 'Will?' she called. 'You all right?'

There was a grunt and a splash, and another oath. His language was taking a battering, she thought with a smile.

'Yes, fine,' he said groggily. 'I'll be out in a minute.'

She hovered, listening to grunts and clonks and the odd cuss, until she heard the creak of a board and a sigh of relief that signalled his safe retreat from the bath.

Heaving a sigh of her own, she retreated with Bruno to the safety of the kitchen, turned on the radio and tried not to think about Will and his delectable naked body while she cleared up after their supper. It didn't work, of course, because she just managed to hit the love-songs happy hour, or that's what it sounded like.

One husky, softly crooned love song after another, all her old favourites, and, of course, she knew the words, so she sang along, misty-eyed and wistful, and for some reason an image of Will kept super-imposing itself on her mental pictures, just to add to the delicious torture.

She wiped down the worktop, humming absently, her mind full of him. He'd looked so—oh, so male, so virile, so incredibly *potent*. A powerful aphrodi-siac. The image was so clear she could have reached out and touched him, felt the smooth silk of his skin, the slight roughness of the hair, the taut, corded mus-cles beneath—

'Oh, hell,' she groaned, throwing the packet of ba-con back into the fridge and trying to put him out of her mind. Not easy. She found herself singing again, the words she knew so well coming naturally to her lips.

Swaying gently to the music, she turned to clear the table, and there he was, standing in the doorway watching her, his face inscrutable.

The song died on her lips. Colour streaming up her cheeks, she turned hastily away, dumping the mugs and plates into the sink and busying herself with the kettle. Lord, she must have looked such a fool! 'Cup of tea?' she suggested briskly, and, stab-bing the 'off' button on the radio she killed the slow, sexy song. In the shocking silence that followed she heard him coming towards her, his bare feet padding softly on the floor.

His voice was deep and husky, right behind her, and made all the little hairs on the nape of her neck stand to attention. 'Please. Could you put this on for me first and take off the plastic bag?'

Reluctantly she turned back to him, avoiding his eyes. Careful not to touch his fingers, she took the support bandage from him and gathered it up to slide it over his left arm. It was still swollen, but less so, the skin discoloured where the bruising had come out. She had an insane urge to kiss it better, and stifled it. She felt enough of an idiot without adding insult to injury.

'How is it?' she asked, easing the support over his fingers and trying still not to touch him.

'Still sore—ouch!'

'Sorry. It would be easier with one of those sleeve things to gather it on.'

'It's fine. Just pull it up. It doesn't hurt that much. I'm just a wimp.'

She gave a soft snort of laughter and eased the bandage into place, smoothing it down with hands that wanted to linger. His arm trembled under her fingertips, and she released it, glad to break the contact that was doing her no good at all.

'Want to do this yourself, or do you want me to do it?' she asked, indicating the shopping bags stuck over the cast to protect it from the water.

'Could you? I tried but I couldn't get the end of the tape.'

'Sure.' She found the end, managed to lift it with her nail and started to peel it off, but he yelped and yanked his arm away.

'Hell, woman! Mind the hairs!' he protested, and she gave him a syrupy smile and took his arm back in an iron grip.

'Now you know how it feels to have your legs

waxed,' she said unsympathetically, and eased off another inch, holding down the hairs with one hand and peeling with the other.

He bore it in grim-lipped silence, and when the bags were off and consigned to the bin, he massaged his sore skin gingerly and gave her a baleful look. 'Next time,' he said clearly, 'we'll use elastic bands.'

She had to turn away to hide the smile. 'How about that cup of tea now?' she said, feeling sorry for him despite herself.

He sighed. 'What I feel like is a damn great Scotch, but I suppose you're going to veto that on medical grounds?'

She arched a brow in surprise. 'Me, with the right of veto? I hardly think so. Since when was I your mother?'

He snorted. 'Doesn't stop you having an opinion on everything else,' he told her bluntly, and she felt a wash of guilty colour sweep her cheeks.

'It's entirely up to you what you do to your body,' she said virtuously. 'Don't hold back on my account.'

'I won't,' he retorted, reaching past her for a glass. He was just lowering it to the worktop when he caught his elbow on the bread crock and the glass slipped from his fingers, shattering on the hard floor.

Bruno rushed forwards to investigate, and as one they turned and yelled, '*No!*' at the poor dog. He stopped in his tracks, and Lucie looked down at Will's bare feet covered in sparkling slivers of glass.

'I should stand right there if I were you,' she told him.

'You don't say,' he murmured drily, and she shot him a look before fetching the dustpan and brush.

She swept carefully around his feet and then went over the whole floor before mopping it to pick up the last tiny shards.

'Right, you can move,' she told him, and with a sigh he sat down at the table and gave a resigned, wry smile.

'I'll settle for tea,' he said, picking a sliver of glass off his foot with his uncooperative right hand. 'God obviously didn't want me to have that Scotch.'

'Apparently not,' Lucie said, returning his smile. She made the tea, put the mugs on the table and they sat together in what could almost have been called companionable silence.

A truce? Wonders will never cease, Lucie thought, but her luck was about to run out. The phone rang, shattering the stillness, and Will answered it.

'For you,' he said, holding out the phone to her.

She took it, puzzled. Who on earth could it be?

'Hello?'

'Lucie? It's me.'

It took her a moment, she was so far away from the reality of London. 'Fergus?' she said, puzzled. 'Hi. How are you?'

Behind her she heard a chair scrape, and Will retreated to the sitting room, the dog following, nails clattering on the bare floor.

The room seemed suddenly empty, and she had to force herself to concentrate on Fergus. He was missing her. He said so, over and over again. He missed her company. He missed her smile. He missed sitting in her flat watching TV. He even missed her temper, he said.

'Do you miss me?' he asked her, and she was shocked to realise that, no, she didn't, not at all. She hadn't given him so much as a passing thought. She made some noncommital reply, and it seemed to satisfy him, probably because his ego was so undentable that he couldn't imagine she wasn't desolate.

'I thought I'd pop down and see you this weekend,' he told her.

'Ah, no. Um. I'm coming to town. I'll see you—I'll ring you from the flat.'

'We'll do lunch.'

'Lovely. I have to go, my tea's getting cold,' she said, and hung up after the briefest of farewells. It was only as she cradled the phone that she realised how cavalier it had sounded.

Poor Fergus. Still, he just wouldn't take the hint.

Her eyes strayed to the sitting-room door, open just a crack. Had Will heard her conversation? And if so, what had he made of it?

And what, in any case, did it matter?

Lucie wasn't sure. She knew one thing, though—it did matter. For some reason that wasn't really clear to her she wanted Will to have a good opinion of her, and it was nothing to do with her professional role and everything to do with a man with a body to die for and the temper of a crotchety rattlesnake.

Oh, dear. She was in big trouble…

CHAPTER FIVE

WILL was annoyed.

Lucie was going back to London for the weekend, and seeing Fergus, whoever the hell Fergus was. It was none of his business, of course, and he kept telling himself that, but it didn't stop it annoying the life out of him all week.

He had a phone call from Pam, to say that Dick had seen the cardiologist and was booked in for angioplasty. The angiogram had shown that he was a suitable candidate, and didn't need the more extensive intervention of open-heart surgery and a bypass operation.

On a professional level Will was pleased for them. On a personal level he was irritated that after all the time he'd spent cajoling Dick, it had been Lucie who'd talked him into taking this final step.

He told himself he was being a child, but she was getting to him. Getting to him in ways he didn't want to think about. Ways that kept him awake at night and then, when he finally slept, coloured his dreams so that even the memory of them made his blood pressure soar.

Crazy, because she drove him mad, but there was just something about her that made him restless and edgy, and made him long for things he couldn't have.

Like her, for instance.

Damn.

He forced himself to concentrate. She was in the

middle of surgery, and he was sitting in, keeping an eye on the time and watching her wheedle and cajole and sympathise and generally make everyone feel better.

Except young Clare Reid, who had come in on Monday with a cough and a disbelieving mother, and was back today with much worse symptoms and a mother who now was berating herself for not listening.

'I knew there was something wrong,' Mrs Reid was saying. 'I can't believe I didn't pay more attention. Whatever is wrong with her?'

Lucie checked through the notes, but the results weren't back. 'I'll check with the lab,' she promised. 'I'll call you back later today, because, I quite agree, it isn't right that she should be feeling so rough.'

Clare coughed again, and Lucie frowned and looked at Will.

'Sounds like whooping cough,' she said thoughtfully, and he frowned. Whooping cough? Although she could have a point...

'Let me ring the lab. If you two could wait outside while Dr Compton sees her next patient, I'll see what I can find out for you, and then we can have you back in and let you know if there's anything to report, OK?'

They nodded, and he went through to another room to make the call.

'Oh, yes, we were just sending that out to you. It's not whooping cough, but it's a related virus. Unfortunately it's not proved susceptible to any of the antivirals. Sorry. Oh, and by the way, it's not notifiable.'

He thanked them and went back to Lucie, and after

she'd finished with her patient, he told her the result.

'So what can we do for her? An anti-viral?'

He shook his head. 'Apparently not. Anyway, I should imagine she's past the acute stage of the illness. Any treatment now will be palliative. I would send her to a good pharmacist for advice on cough remedies, and tell her to sit in a hot, steamy bath and hang wet towels on her radiator at night and sniff Olbas oil.'

'Gorgeous. I wonder if she was still infectious on Monday?' Lucie said drily, and he grinned despite himself.

'Maybe. If so, knowing how my luck's running at the moment, I'll get it. All I need now is a good dose of mumps or chickenpox and my happiness will be complete.'

Lucie chuckled, and he looked at her and thought how incredibly sexy she was with that wide smile and her eyes crinkling with humour. It was just such a hell of a shame they weren't like this with each other all the time, but they weren't. For some reason he couldn't fathom, they seemed to rub each other up the wrong way the entire time.

He stifled a sigh. Probably just as well, really. He didn't need any more complications in his life, particularly not complications that he had to work with, and, like it or not, he and Lucie were stuck with each other for almost six more months.

And, he reminded himself, she was about to go back to London for the weekend to Fergus. Good. He'd have the house to himself again.

Bliss.

*   *   *

The flat seemed incredibly noisy. Lucie packed up the remainder of her things, and put what she didn't want with her into a cupboard in her room.

Her flatmate's partner was moving in—well, had moved in, more or less, some time ago, and was officially taking over her portion of the rent now, which was a relief. It also meant she could come back and stay for a while until she found another place, and she'd have a bolt-hole if necessary.

And it might well be necessary if Will Ryan was as grumpy for the next six months as he'd been for the last week. She sighed and threw the last few things into a case, clipped it shut and stood it by the wall. She didn't want to put it in her car until she left. Security wasn't London's strong point, and there was no point tempting fate.

She rang Fergus to arrange to meet for lunch, and he was round within minutes. Not quite what she'd had in mind, but he'd insisted on escorting her to their venue.

He spoiled her. He was rich enough to do it, but still, he spoiled her and took her to one of those exclusive places where you had to book weeks in advance. A man of power and influence, she thought with humour, but it didn't influence her at all. All the pomp and ceremony and discreet yet ostentatious service just got on her nerves, and she found herself thinking of eating bacon sandwiches in the kitchen with Will.

Not a good start to their lunch. Lucie forced herself to concentrate on Fergus, and realised that he was talking about himself as usual.

Finally, as they pushed aside the remains of their dark chocolate baskets with summer fruits in Kirch, topped with a delicate trail of cream and chocolate sauce in a puddle of raspberry coulis garnished with a sprig of mint, Fergus asked about her.

'So, how's life in the boonies?' he said, sitting back with an indulgent smile. 'I've missed you, you know.'

'You said—and it's fine,' she lied. 'There's a horse that grazes outside my bedroom window, and a dog called Bruno and a cat called Minnie—and my trainer's fallen off a ladder and broken his arm, so at the moment I'm helping him out a bit in the evenings and doing all the driving to work and back.'

'Poor old boy,' Fergus said kindly, and Lucie thought of Will, dark and irritable and pacing round like a wounded grizzly, and stifled a smile. Poor old boy? Not in this lifetime! Still, she didn't bother to correct Fergus. If he realised that Will was only thirty-three, he'd be down there like a shot, getting possessive and territorial, and Lucie would be forced to kill him.

And that would stuff up her Hippocratic oath and probably interfere more than a little with the progress of her career.

Oh, well. She'd have to keep them apart, which was no hardship. She couldn't see Fergus on Will's farm, picking his way through the puddles and pushing the dog aside when he was muddy and bouncy and over-enthusiastic—and for some reason she didn't care to analyse, she didn't want Fergus there anyway.

'So, how are the patients? Do they all chew straw and say, "Ooh, aa-rr"?' Fergus asked her with a patronising smile.

She thought of Pam and Dick, lovely people—

people she'd been able to help by her presence there. 'Only half of them. The others are mostly inarticulate.'

He laughed as if she'd told the funniest joke in the world, and she sighed. She really couldn't be bothered with this.

'Fergus, it's been a lovely lunch,' she began, but he wasn't one to pick up subtle hints.

'And it's not over,' he announced proudly. 'I thought we could go back to my flat for coffee, and then I thought we could take a stroll through St James's Park, and then tonight I thought we could take in a show—there's that new one that's just opened with rave reviews. I'm sure I can get tickets.'

She was sure he could, too, but she wasn't interested.

'Fergus, I don't really have time,' she told him. 'I have to get back to Suffolk tonight—I'm on duty tomorrow.'

She waited for the lightning bolt to strike her down, but it didn't come. It should. She was starting to tell so many lies. She ought to just say, Look, Fergus, you're a nice man but not for me.

Actually, she had said it! She'd said it over and over again. Most recently last weekend, just before she'd left for Suffolk.

Blast.

'Perhaps next weekend,' he coaxed, and she sighed.

'I can't.'

'Then I'll come to you. I'll fit in round you. I'll buy some wellies and take a stroll while you're busy, and we can find a restaurant and eat out in the evening. I assume they do *have* restaurants?'

'I'm sure we can find a fish-and-chip shop,' she said drily, and he recoiled. Oh, lord, how had she ever let him talk her into this?

She realised with a sense of shock that she was feeling defensive about his attitude—an attitude she'd shared until this last week. How strange.

'I really have to go—I've still got a lot of clearing up to do at the flat before I leave,' she told him, adding another lie to the heap that teetered on the funeral pyre of her conscience.

'Wait for me. I'll pay the bill and take you back.'

'No, don't,' she said, hastily pushing him back into his chair. 'You stay and have coffee, and I'll get on. I've got some shopping to do on the way back.'

She stooped and kissed his cheek, thanked him again and made her escape into the fresh air, or what passed for it in London. She inhaled deeply. It was familiar and comforting, but somehow strange.

She went back to her flat, made coffee and waited till she thought she'd given her glass of wine time to clear her system, then left a note for her flatmate, threw her stuff into the car and headed back to Suffolk and Will.

The house seemed empty. At first Will revelled in the silence, listening to the songs of the birds and the gentle snort of Henry outside the window. Then, after he'd struggled to wash and dress, he went down to the kitchen and looked around for something easy to eat.

Cereal, he thought, and sat at the table with nothing to break the silence but the crunching of corn-flakes and the sigh of the dog. No Lucie humming as she pottered, or chattering brightly about nothing in particular.

It was good, he told himself, but a sliver of loneliness sneaked in and made him restless. He went over to the cottage and let himself in, opening the windows and letting the air circulate. He'd had the old bed and carpet collected and taken away during the week, but the room still smelled musty, and today a man was coming to paint the ceiling.

His incapacity infuriated him. He was perfectly capable of doing all the things he'd just had to pay good money to have done, and much worse than that was having to rely on Lucie for his transport.

He went into the sitting room and looked around. She'd brought some of her things in here last weekend and stacked them in an untidy heap on one side, and he had a burning urge to know what she considered essential. A jumper spilled out of a carrier bag, a belt hung out of the side of a suitcase. And there, in a bag at the back, was a dog-eared teddy bear.

He found himself smiling, and frowned. It wasn't funny. She was hopelessly disorganised, and he had to turn her into a GP. What chance was there? She had to be highly ordered and disciplined to work in a modern practice with all the rules and regulations that applied.

Her cheerful disregard for convention might be all very well in a musician or an artist, but in a doctor it was a recipe for disaster.

Still frowning, he went back to the bedroom and sniffed. Not too bad. The clouds looked a bit threatening, so he closed the windows again, except for the little fanlight, and crossed the yard to his house. Amanda drew up just before he gained the safety of the back door, and bounded out of the car, waving cheerfully.

'Hi! How are you?' she asked, bearing down on him.

He sighed inwardly. 'Better, thanks. My left hand's almost back to normal,' he told her, waggling it rather further than it wanted to go and smiling to cover the wince. 'See? All but fixed.'

'Anything I can do? Shopping, cooking—washing?'

He thought of his back in the bath and nearly choked. 'No, no, it's fine,' he said hastily. 'I've got everything I need, and Lucie did my washing before she went away.'

Amanda's face brightened. 'She's gone?'

'Only for the weekend,' he corrected quickly. 'Just to sort out her flat.'

Her face fell again. 'Oh, well. If there's anything I can do, just holler.'

'I will. Thanks.' He retreated inside, closing the door with indecent haste, and sank down at the kitchen table. 'She's getting worse, Bruno,' he told the dog in an undertone. 'What are we going to do?'

Bruno wagged his tail, looking hopeful. 'Come on, then,' he said, relenting, and with a lot of wiggling and shoving and swearing he managed to get his boots on. They headed off down the track to the woods, turned left and followed the little path down through the edge of the wood amongst the bluebells.

It was beautiful, peaceful and still and restoring. He felt the tranquillity easing back into him, and, tucking his right hand into the pocket of his jacket, he strolled along, breathing in the cool, fresh air and listening to the sounds of the countryside while

Bruno fossicked in the undergrowth and chased interesting smells and the odd rabbit.

They reached the edge of the river and he sat down on a stone, ignoring the creeping damp and absorbing the glorious views. The sun was high now, and its warmth caressed his face and seeped through his jacket, driving out the chill.

Bliss. What more could a man possibly want?

Someone to share it with?

'Bruno!' he called, standing abruptly and heading back. He had someone to share it with—someone loyal and devoted and emotionally undemanding.

Well, perhaps not loyal. The mutt had spent the week on Lucie's bed, proving his fickle nature. Just because she was feeding him whole suppers, of course. He'd be her friend for life because of that.

He wondered what Lucie was doing now and who'd slept with her last night.

Fergus?

A writhing knot of something that surely wasn't jealousy wrapped itself around his gut and squeezed. Ridiculous. It was entirely her own business who she slept with!

He went back to the house, hooked his boots off and stomped upstairs. He really ought to be getting on with this room, he thought, and opened the door.

Frustration hit him like a fist in the chest. It would be weeks—months, probably—before he could get back to work in here.

Slamming the door, he went back downstairs and over to the cottage. Pete had arrived and set up his dustsheets, and was priming the ceiling so the damp mark didn't bleed through the new paint.

'Come and have a coffee while that dries,' he suggested, and Pete nodded.

'Will do, mate. Give us a few more minutes.'

'OK.'

Will went back to the kitchen and stared morosely at the washing-up in the sink. Lucie had bought him some huge rubber gloves that he could just about get on over the cast and support bandage, but putting them on was an act that required more patience than he would find in his lifetime, and he gave up. The washing up could wait. She'd be back tomorrow.

Late, probably, and overtired from her activities with Fergus.

'Fergus.' He spat the name, realising he was beginning to hate the man without any justification. Irrational, stupid behavior, he told himself, but the thought of someone—anyone—touching Lucie intimately made him want to kill.

Which was totally ridiculous, because there was no way he wanted her.

Was there?

It had been a lovely day, Lucie realised in surprise. Odd, how insulated from the weather she'd been in London. Much less aware.

Now, driving back down the once-unnerving track towards the house, she wound down the window and breathed in deeply. Something was flowering, and the heady scent wafted through the window. It was gorgeous. Humming to herself, she turned into the farmyard and saw a man in white overalls sitting on the steps by the back door, drinking tea.

Not Will. Her eyes scanned the yard, irrationally disappointed to find him missing, and then he came out of the back door armed with a biscuit tin, and she felt an involuntary smile curve the corners of her mouth.

He lifted one hand in a wave, and she pulled up outside the cottage and got out, strolling over. No London strut, no rush, no hurry, just an amble in the evening sun.

'Hi.'

'You're back early,' Will said, sounding almost accusing. 'I wasn't expecting you till tomorrow.'

Damn. He'd probably planned a quiet evening with a woman, she thought, and felt a soft tide of colour invade her cheeks. 'I'll keep out of the way,' she promised. 'If that's all right. Clearing up the flat didn't take as long as I thought.'

And for some reason she couldn't get away from Fergus quick enough.

'It's fine,' Will said shortly, leaving her with the distinct impression that it was far from fine and it was only good manners that prevented him from telling her where to go.

'Is it all right to put my things straight into the cottage?' she asked, and the man in the white overalls tipped back his baseball cap with one finger and shot her a searching look.

'Mind the bedroom—ceiling's wet and the air might be a bit damp for an hour or two.'

'I'll use the sitting room,' she promised, and since there was no offer of a cup of tea forthcoming, she took herself off and unloaded her car while they sat on the steps and watched her struggle.

Not that Will could do anything, but he could at least have put the kettle on, she thought.

And to think she'd been looking forward to coming back!

By Monday morning Lucie was ready to kill Will. He'd been remote and surly all weekend, and she'd got the distinct impression he was cross with her—but why? He'd said—so firmly that she'd dropped the subject like a hot brick—that she wasn't interfering with his plans.

Perhaps he was just in pain. He'd probably decided he didn't need pills any more, and she was the one to catch the flak. Well, damn him.

By the time they were ready for work he was as crotchety as a bear with a sore head, and when he went outside and sat firmly in the passenger seat of the Volvo, she couldn't be bothered to argue. She got the distinct impression he was spoiling for a fight, and she was damned if she was going to give him one!

Instead she smiled meekly, slid behind the wheel and drove up the track as if she were carrying a nuclear warhead in the back. He shot her a suspicious look, folded his arms across his chest and winced as he bent his left wrist.

Out of the corner of her eye she saw him shuffling his arms uncomfortably, and had to suppress her sympathy. He was being crabby and ungracious, and she had no intention of feeling sorry for him!

Her surgery got off to a flying start with the return of Mr Gregory, her overweight patient who was trying to lose weight and was suffering from indigestion. His pain was worse, and Lucie decided to take the bull by the horns.

'Have you had an ECG recently?' she asked, taking his blood pressure.

'No. Can't say I've ever had one,' he told her.

'Right. Just to eliminate it from our enquiries, then, I'd like you to see the nurse and have an ECG done, and we'll also get her to take some bloods to test for *Helicobacter pylori*.'

'Is that the gastric ulcer bug? A friend of mine had that not so long ago.'

'Really?' Lucie said, thoughtful. 'Is it possible you picked it up in the same place?'

'Maybe. We teach in the same school, and we went on a school trip together. The food was pretty rough.'

'I think it's hygiene rather than quality that matters, but it's possible it came from there. It can give painful symptoms. And while we wait for the results of that we can give you a drug to suppress the symptoms so you don't feel so bad. OK? So if you go and see the nurse, she can get it all under way, and I'll give you a prescription now for the thing to reduce your stomach acid. You should be much more comfortable.'

'So you don't think it's my heart, then?'

She shook her head. 'No, I don't, but I have to be sure. I can't just hope, I have to know, and so do you.'

He stood up. 'Thanks, Doc. When do I see you again?'

She looked at Will. 'How soon do the results come back?'

'Leave it a week,' he advised. 'They should be back then.'

'Next Monday, then,' Lucie suggested, and Mr Gregory nodded.

'Will do. Thanks again.'

She waited, after the door closed, for Will to comment, but he didn't. To her surprise, when she turned round he was slowly writing a comment on a piece of paper. Later, then, she thought, and sighed. Oh, well.

The carpet was down, the bed was in and Lucie was moving out.

Will gave her the bedding out of the little airing cupboard in the cottage, and watched her make the bed. It was a mistake. She ran a slender, capable hand over the sheet, smoothing it flat, and he imagined feeling its texture on his skin.

She plumped the pillows, dropped them in place, straightened and smiled at him, and he felt the heat balloon inside him.

'I'd help you with the quilt but I'm not sure I can be much use,' he said gruffly, and she shrugged and smiled again.

'It's not a problem. I can cope. Shall we christen the kettle?'

And he realised that he would get his kitchen back to himself now. No more cosy chats over tea, no more bickering over the menu or skiving off the washing-up.

No more radio. That was a plus.

No more Lucie singing along to it with that slightly husky voice. That had to be a plus—didn't it?

He went and put the kettle on, as much to distance himself from Lucie and the bed as anything. There wasn't any milk, and there were no teabags or coffee granules, so he went over to his house and brought a selection of bits and pieces to start her off.

By the time the kettle boiled, she was in the kitchen looking hopeful, and he took two mugs down awkwardly with his left hand and looked at her.

'Tea or coffee?'

'Is there a choice?'

'I've even brought you over some hot chocolate.'

Her smile seemed to light up the room, and it touched his heart. 'Oh, thanks. I ought to go shopping. I could do that now, actually, when we've had our tea. You could probably do with some stocking up, as well, couldn't you?'

'Probably. So did you want tea, or was that a figure of speech?'

'Tea. I'll make it, you sit down.'

So he sank gratefully into one of the comfy armchairs and waited, and a moment later she came round the corner from the kitchen area with two mugs and curled herself up in the other chair opposite him, her feet tucked up under her bottom and her nose buried in the mug.

It was so ridiculously homely and cosy that he nearly laughed, but it would have been a cynical, bitter laugh and she didn't deserve it. He wasn't sure why he felt like that, anyway. Frustration? Probably.

And now he was going to have to endure the joys of the supermarket with her. Wonderful. He scowled into his tea.

'Is it all right?' Lucie asked, and he looked up.

'What?'

'The tea. Is it all right? You gave it such a look.'

He laughed self-consciously. 'It's fine. Sorry. I was thinking about something else.'

'Lord, I hope it wasn't me,' she said with her husky chuckle.

'No,' he denied, and realised it was probably true. It wasn't so much Lucie as what she represented that was making him edgy and restless. He drank the tea too hot, and unfolded himself from the chair.

'I'll get ready for the supermarket.'

'Oh, you don't have to go!' she exclaimed. 'You look tired. Why don't you give me a list and stay here and have a rest? I'll get your shopping. You can owe me.'

And then, perversely, he felt disappointed.

Lucie screwed up her eyebrows and peered at his list. What on earth did that say? She should have asked him to translate. She had the distinct feeling that his writing was awful when he had a functioning arm. Now it was atrocious.

Liver? She shuddered gently, but it was on his list. OK, liver, then. She looked in the chiller cabinet, fished out what looked as if it might be the right sort and volume, and dropped it in the trolley. Gross.

She moved on, shaking her head over his list on several more occasions, and finally she reached the end. Oh, well, what she didn't have she—or he— could manage without for another day or two. She was tired, and she wanted to get settled into the cottage.

She was looking forward to being herself, to relaxing and not having to worry about disturbing Will, or doing any of the thousands of things that seemed to make him scowl.

*   *   *

'Liver?'

'It was on your list.'

'Was it, hell. Show me.'

She pulled the list out of her pocket and thrust it under his nose. 'See? Liver.'

'Limes,' he corrected with a short sigh. 'It says limes.'

She looked at him as if he'd grown two heads. 'Limes? Why on earth would you want limes?'

'To squeeze over grilled chicken breasts, with salad. I just fancied some. I *hate* liver.'

A smile lit up her face. 'Hey, we agree on something,' she said cheerfully. 'Never mind, I'm sure Bruno likes liver.'

Will gave the dog a disgusted look. 'I'm sure he does. Are you certain you two aren't in league?'

She took out the rest of his shopping while he watched and commented, and then handed him the bill. 'Charge the dog for the liver,' she advised, and then headed for the door. 'I'm just going to put my shopping away, and I'll be back for my overnight things.'

He nodded and watched her go, and then found himself standing at the window, watching her across the yard. The curtains in the cottage were open, and he could see her moving around, putting her shopping away in the cupboards and the fridge.

Liver, he thought disgustedly, and caught the dog's eye. 'Definitely in cahoots,' he growled, and Bruno wagged his tail cheerfully.

'You're going to have to sleep with me tonight, sport, and don't get any ideas about lying on the bed, either. She's spoiled you.'

The dog woofed softly, and Will relented and

scratched his ears. 'You're a good boy, really,' he murmured, and the dog collapsed on the floor at his feet, quite content. He went back to watching Lucie, and a few moments later he saw her crossing the yard.

She came in with a smile, and ran upstairs, returning a few minutes later with an armful of clothes and her washbag. 'I can get the rest tomorrow. I want to unpack some things tonight.'

He nodded, and then there was an awkward pause.

'Thank you for putting up with me until the cottage was done,' she said softly, and he felt churlish for his resentment.

'It's been a pleasure,' he said, and she laughed.

'Liar.'

He looked down at his hands. 'No, really. You've been very kind while I've been out of action. You've done all sorts of things for me. I'm sorry I haven't been more grateful. I just—I'm usually pretty self-sufficient and it comes a bit hard having to rely on someone else.'

He looked up again, and their eyes locked. 'I'll help you over there—you've got your hands rather full to open the doors.'

'Oh—thanks.'

At the door of the cottage he paused, curiously unwilling to go in. 'I'll leave you to it,' he said gruffly, and she went up on tiptoe and kissed his cheek.

'Thanks,' she murmured.

'Any time,' he said, and then something shifted, tilting the world on its axis. For a moment neither of them moved, and then as if in slow motion he lowered his head and kissed her lips.

For a second they both froze, and then she melted, her mouth soft and yielding, and he could taste her. Heat shot through him, shocking him, and he drew away.

'Goodnight, Lucie,' he said, his voice husky with the desire that was ripping through him, and he backed away, turning on his heel and striding away from her, towards his house and sanity.

He didn't look back.

CHAPTER SIX

LUCIE watched Will go, striding away from her as if she might give him some terrible disease. And yet his kiss had been so tender, so gentle and coaxing— so unlike him.

At first. Then it had taken off, and she'd wanted to hold him, but her arms had still been clutching the clothes in front of her, so that the only point of contact had been their fevered mouths.

The heat had threatened to consume her, but it had been over in seconds, so brief that now she could hardly believe it had happened, and Will had pulled away, his face stunned.

That he hadn't meant the kiss to happen was obvious. What was less obvious to Lucie was why it had been such a beautiful and tender kiss. A cherishing kiss. A needy kiss. Lord, so needy...

Lucie swallowed hard, turned and pushed the door shut behind her, heading for the bedroom. The clothes had to be hung up, her wash things put away in the bathroom, and she could do with sorting out some of her other clothes that had been in a suitcase all week.

Nevertheless, she sank down on the edge of the newly made bed, the clothes still in her arms, and relived the touch of Will's mouth on hers. She could still feel the imprint of his lips, the soft velvet texture so at odds with the slight rasp of his chin.

He'd angled his mouth over hers, taking advantage

of her willing response to deepen the kiss, and it had grown a little wild then, suddenly. Until he'd pulled away.

Perhaps it was just as well she'd moved out of the house and wasn't going to be exposed to him crossing the landing to the bathroom in nothing more than a pair of jogging bottoms hanging loosely on his hips!

Too much sex appeal for comfort, Lucie thought, and for some reason she had an image of Fergus— bland, mild-mannered, successful and totally without that edge that made Will so very tempting. Fergus was safe—and Lucie realised with some astonishment that she didn't want to be safe. She was sick of being safe. She'd been safe too long, and now she wanted more.

She wanted Will.

It was equally clear to her, however, that Will didn't want her—or, rather, that he didn't *want* to want her. Because he did want her, that much she was utterly sure of.

A thread of excitement wove itself along her veins, and she stood up, humming softly to herself, and put her clothes away, then started on her boxes. She pottered for ages, quietly working through the strange collection of things she'd acquired over the years, and thinking of Will.

Finally the room was clear and she could find a chair to sit in, so she made a hot drink and curled up in the chair with the TV on and watched the late news. She could see Will's house through the window, and after a while she heard him calling Bruno, then the kitchen light went off and a few moments later the bedroom light went on.

She wondered how he was coping, and if there was anything he couldn't manage to do for himself. She should have offered to help him still, but she'd got the distinct impression he'd wanted her out as quickly as possible.

No wonder, if all that heat was steaming gently under his collar the entire time! She turned off the television and got ready for bed, enjoying the privacy of a house of her own for the very first time.

Well, sort of enjoying it. It seemed terribly quiet, with not even so much as a passing car to break the silence, and every creak seemed curiously sinister. She wondered what Will was thinking, and if he, too, was remembering their kiss.

She climbed into bed and picked up her diary off the bedside table. She had more than a week's worth to write up, and with all that had happened she was going to be up all night doing it. What on earth had possessed her to pack it?

She wrote furiously, and finally arrived at today's entry. She wrote, 'He kissed me. Don't think he meant to. Don't think he means to do it again—we'll have to see about that! I have a feeling he needs rescuing from himself. It can be my next challenge—RESCUING DR RYAN.'

With a smile on her lips, she put the diary down, turned out the light and snuggled under the quilt, falling asleep almost instantly.

Will had hardly slept a wink. Bruno had insisted on lying across his feet, so he'd woken with two more compromised limbs and a deep and abiding hatred of things canine.

He washed and dressed with difficulty, fed the dog

and cat and pulled on a coat, shoving his feet into his boots. 'Come on, pest,' he said to Bruno, who was still fruitlessly chasing his empty bowl around the floor. 'Let's go and see the river—*if* I can walk that far.'

Bruno, blissfully unaware of his master's sarcasm, shot out of the back door and ran over to the cottage, then sat whining by the door. Will sighed.

'Get in the queue,' he muttered, and turned towards the track. 'Come on, dog. We don't have women in our lives—remember?'

After a last, lingering look at the door, Bruno turned and trotted obediently at his side all the way down to the river and back, cheerfully retrieving dead goodness-knows-whats and presenting them to Will. And gradually the dawning of a beautiful day drove out the blues and restored the peace in his soul, and he wandered back to the house with Bruno in tow. The dog had brought home a souvenir, a festering bit of rabbit leg dangling from his jaws, and he offered it to Will with a grin.

'You're revolting,' he said disparagingly, just as they turned the corner and found Lucie poised at the back door of his house. She looked at the dog and her eyes widened.

'Yuck, Bruno, that's foul! You horrid dog!'

'He's just being a dog. They are foul. Have you got a problem with the cottage?'

She shook her head. 'No. I just thought I ought to pop over and see if there was anything you needed help with—you know, with your arms and everything.'

A genuine offer? Or any feeble excuse to interfere in his life?

How could he tell? He couldn't, so he played safe.

'I'm fine,' he said, possibly a bit shortly, and after a second's startled hesitation she ran down the steps to the yard and gave him a fleeting little smile.

'That's OK, then. Shout if you need anything. I'll be ready to go in twenty minutes.'

And she was gone, all but running round the corner and leaving him nursing a massive guilt trip and a whole truckload of resentment as a result.

Hell. Life had been much simpler before he'd met her!

The rest of the week passed. That was all Lucie could say. The days were sometimes easy, sometimes difficult. The evenings were long and lonely, and the nights—she didn't want to think about the nights. Suffice it to say Will featured extensively in her dreams, and she began to wonder if she'd bitten off more than she could chew with her challenge to rescue him. Certainly she didn't seem to be making any progress.

Nor did her first patient on Friday morning. Mr Gregory's stomach was still proving a problem, pending the result of his blood test, but at least the ECG had proved normal, as she'd expected.

'I think I ought to start him on the treatment,' Lucie said to Will thoughtfully, just before Mr Gregory came in. 'If he's back because it's worse, I have to do something.'

'The treatment's very expensive, and might mask other symptoms,' he warned.

'So what would you do?'

He leant back in his chair, steepled his fingers and pressed them against his lips, peering at her thoughtfully. 'I don't know. Encourage him to wait and give the palliative treatment which was all we had until a short while ago.'

'I've done that. He's coming back. There must be a reason.'

Will shrugged. 'Reassure him. I think he's worried. We'll see.'

Will was right, of course. He was just worried and wanted reassurance that it wasn't, in fact, his heart. Finally satisfied that he was in no danger, Mr Gregory left, and Lucie finished her surgery without any further complications. She was just about to leave on her calls when the receptionist took a call from an anxious mother whose seventeen-year-old daughter was vomiting and looking very peaky.

'We'll call in—we have to go that way,' Will told the receptionist. 'I doubt if it's anything urgent—probably a hangover.'

'Sceptic,' Lucie said with a chuckle, and his mouth cracked into a fleeting smile.

'Absolutely. That's the modern youth for you. No restraint and no stamina.'

Lucie shook her head, stifling the smile. 'Such a sweeping generalisation. I bet you were really wild at university.'

A wry grin tilted his lips. 'I had my moments, I confess—although nothing like they get up to these days.'

'Ah, poor old man,' she teased, and he snorted.

'Can we get on, please? We've got another call to fit in now and, hangover or not, it'll take time.' He scooped up the notes in his right hand, and Lucie noticed that it seemed to be co-operating fairly well.

He'd been using it much more in the last few days, and it was obviously less painful.

Not good enough, though, that he could drive yet, and she could tell that was frustrating him. Will went out to the car park, went round to the driver's side, swore colourfully under his breath and went round to the passenger side instead.

'When can you drive?' she asked him, and he glowered at her over the roof of the car.

'Not until the cast is off. I always advise my patients not to drive until they've had the cast off and their arms are functioning normally without undue pain. It's for insurance reasons, really.'

'So I suppose you ought to take your own advice.'

He snorted. 'Very probably.'

'Mmm,' she agreed, sucking in her cheeks and ducking behind the wheel before he could see the smile that was sure to show in her eyes.

He appeared beside her, shooting her an unreadable look. 'In the meantime,' he continued, 'you're stuck with me, and vice versa, so we might as well both make the best of it.'

He then proceeded to spend the entire journey telling her she was in the wrong lane or had missed a turning.

'For God's sake, didn't you see that cyclist?' he yelled as they neared their destination, and she glowered at him and turned on the radio. Anything was preferable to listening to him ranting!

'Do we have to have that on?'

She pulled over, switched off the engine and turned to face him. 'Will, I am an adult,' she said with exaggerated patience. 'I have a current, valid, clean driving licence. I do not need you giving me a hard time just because you want to be able to drive and can't! I've been driving for ten years and I've never had an accident or been pulled up by the police.'

'That's a miracle!'

'And I don't need you telling me how to do everything all the time!' she finished. 'Now, either we're going to do this in my car, or you're going to shut up, because frankly I've had enough!'

He turned away, letting out a short, harsh sigh and glaring hard enough to melt the glass. 'I'm sorry,' he said gruffly, and she nearly choked. An apology? From Will?

'Thank you,' she replied, struggling for a humble tone. 'Now, where do you want me to go from here—apart from hell?'

He turned and met her eyes, and gave a rueful grin. 'It's not personal,' he confessed. 'I just can't delegate—and I hate being driven. The only accident I've ever been in, someone else was driving. I find it hard not being in control.'

'That's because you're a control freak,' Lucie told him drily. 'If it's any help, I passed first time and I've taken my advanced driving test as well.'

'And passed?' he asked her, picking up on her careful phrasing.

She grinned. 'Not exactly—but I didn't fail drastically.'

He gave a soft snort and shook his head, but the tension was gone, and at least the atmosphere in the car was restored.

'So, where to, boss?' she asked again, and he directed her, and for the rest of the journey he kept his mouth firmly shut.

They arrived at the house of the girl with the 'hangover', and her mother opened the door.

'Mrs Webb? I'm Dr Lucie Compton, and I'm covering for Dr Ryan at the moment. I've come to see Harriet.'

'Oh, I am glad you're here. She's looking awful. Come on up.' She led them to a bedroom where a thin, pale girl lay under a quilt, looking extremely unwell. Her skin was waxy, her eyes were sunken and she looked exhausted. It was certainly more than a simple hangover.

'This is Harriet,' her mother said. 'Harriet, darling, it's the doctor.'

Lucie smiled at her gently and crouched down beside the bed. 'Hello, I'm Lucie Compton, and this is Dr Ryan,' she told the girl. 'I'm covering his patients at the moment. Can you tell me how you're feeling?'

'Sick,' Harriet said weakly. 'So sick. I never feel very hungry, but just now I feel really ill if I eat.'

'Are you being sick?' Lucie asked her.

She nodded. 'A bit. Not enough. I feel I want to do more, but all I can do is retch.'

'Any diarrhoea, or constipation? Any other tummy problems?'

Harriet shook her head. 'Not really.'

'Mind if I have a look at your tummy?' Lucie asked, and at a nod from Harriet she peeled back the quilt.

In contrast to her thin face and arms, her abdomen seemed bloated, and Lucie lifted her nightshirt out of the way and examined the skin. There was no sign of abnormal colouration, no hot spots or rashes, but there was a definite mass in the midline, consistent with an aortic aneurysm or an intestinal obstruction.

'Are you bringing up any blood?' Lucie asked, feeling round the margins of the mass.

'A little—sort of streaks of it.'

'Red, or brown?'

'Oh—I don't know. Maybe both. Brown gritty bits sometimes.'

Lucie shot a look over her shoulder at Will. 'How good are your hands? I'd like a second opinion.'

'I'm sure I can manage,' he murmured, and, bending over Harriet, he worked his way over the mass, his fingers probing gently. A fleeting frown crossed his brow, and he quirked an eyebrow at Lucie.

'It feels like a mass in the stomach,' he said, confirming her fears, and Lucie nodded.

She scanned Harriet's hair, and, yes, it seemed thin and wispy.

'Harriet, have you ever eaten your hair?' she asked gently.

'Oh, no!' her mother said. 'She used to, when she was tiny, so she always had it short. Right up until two years ago, but we thought she'd outgrown it.'

'I have!' Harriet protested feebly. 'I don't do it any more, I swear!'

'You might be doing it in your sleep,' Will suggested. 'It happens, especially during times of stress, and I imagine you're doing the first year of your A-levels?'

Harriet nodded. 'Yes—and I have been worried. Do you think I've got a hairball or something?'

'Very possibly,' Lucie confirmed. 'I think you need to go to hospital for investigation, and if we're right, you'll have to have it removed. They'll know the best way of doing it. I'll contact the hospital now and get you admitted. Is that all right, Mrs Webb?'

Mrs Webb was sitting down on the end of the bed, looking shocked. 'A hairball?'

'The correct term is a trichobezoar,' Will explained. 'It's very rare, but the fact that she used to eat her hair points to it being highly likely in the light of her other symptoms. We do need to get it checked out as a matter of urgency, though.'

'So should I take her in now?'

Will shook his head. 'I would suggest we call an ambulance and admit her direct to the surgical team on take, and they can decide what they want to do. If you take her in yourself, you'll have to queue through Accident and Emergency, which isn't a good idea with Harriet feeling so unwell.'

'Mum,' Harriet said feebly, and Mrs Webb moved up the bed and put her arms round her distressed daughter.

'It's all right, darling. It'll be all right.'

'I thought I'd stopped!' she wept, and then started to retch again.

Will looked at Lucie. 'I think we need to mobilise the ambulance,' he said in an undertone. 'She's very weak, and I don't like the feel of that mass. It's utterly rigid and very large. I think her stomach's within an inch of rupture.'

'Me, too. Can I leave it to you to talk to them? You know who to refer to.'

He nodded. 'Mrs Webb, may I use your phone, please?' he asked, and she looked up.

'Oh. Yes, of course. There's one in the front bedroom, by the bed.'

He went out, and Lucie stayed with them, telling them more about the tests that might be performed and getting a little more history. She made some notes for the receiving surgical team, and by the time the ambulance arrived Harriet's bag was packed and Mrs Webb had contacted her husband and explained what was going on.

They all left together, Harriet and her mother in the ambulance, Lucie and Will to their next case, and as soon as they were out of earshot Lucie let out her breath in a rush.

'Wow. I've never seen anything like it,' she confessed.

'Nor have I. It's very rare, but there was a tragic case not all that long ago. I think it's all part and parcel of the pressure we put kids under. Look at Clare Reid, worrying because her father will be cross if she's sick and doesn't do well in her end-of-year exams. But this, I have to say, is much more serious. I wonder if she's got psychiatric history. Let me look in the notes.'

He fumbled through them as Lucie drove, checking through the early correspondence, and then stabbed the paper with a triumphant finger. 'Yup. Here it is. Trichotillomania—hair pulling and eating. Age five. Psychiatric referral, discharged six months later—presumably after she was ''cured'' with a haircut. Poor kid.'

'Do you think she'll make it?' Lucie asked, dwelling on the terrified mother's face. She, too, had probably seen the news a couple of years ago about the teenager who had died with the condition. It must have struck fear into her heart, and rightly so, given her daughter's history.

'I hope so,' Will said heavily. 'She looks pretty grim, though, and she's obviously lost quite a bit of blood over recent weeks. She's as white as a sheet.

Still, hopefully we were called in time and they'll be able to do something if the inside of her stomach isn't too raw and vulnerable to haemorrhage.'

If.

Their next few calls were much more routine—a case of tonsillitis which could easily have been brought to the surgery, a fall in an elderly lady which had resulted in stiffness and soreness, not surprisingly, a baby with diarrhoea and vomiting who was getting dehydrated but had actually started keeping some boiled water down by the time they arrived. Lucie gave the mother some sachets of electrolyte replacement, and instructions that if the baby didn't pick up by four, they were to be called out again and the baby might have to be admitted to hospital for rehydration.

Then they went back, dealt with the correspondence and notes from the week, had a meeting about practice policy on drug offenders and then while Lucie did the evening surgery, Will called the hospital about Harriet Webb.

He popped his head round the door between patients. 'Harriet's all right—they've removed a massive hairball but they think her stomach will heal. Amazingly it didn't look too bad. She's had a blood transfusion and she's holding well.'

Lucie felt her shoulders drop a few inches, and laughed. 'Excellent. I really wasn't sure she'd make it.'

'Nor was I. How many more have you got?'

'Three—I won't be long.'

'Take your time. I'll have a cup of tea—do you want one?'

'I'll wait,' she said with a shake of her head. 'I'd rather get home.'

He nodded and left her to it, and half an hour later they were on their way.

'Any plans for the weekend?' Will asked her, and she had a sudden chill. Fergus had said he'd come down, but he hadn't contacted her, thank God. Maybe he'd taken the hint from her abrupt departure after lunch on Saturday.

'Not really,' she said evasively. 'How about you?'

He shrugged. 'What can I do? Sit about and fret because I can't get on? Walk the dog till his legs fall off? You tell me.'

'What would you normally have been doing?' she asked.

His laugh was short and wry. 'The house? In case you haven't noticed it's barely habitable. I've done the roof and the dampproofing and started with the kitchen and breakfast room and two bedrooms and some basic plumbing, but nothing's finished, and the rest of it is crying out for some progress. The only rooms that are virtually done are the two bedrooms, and they just need decorating.'

'Why on earth,' she asked, negotiating the track carefully, 'did you take on something so challenging?'

'Because I like a challenge? Because I wanted to live here and it was falling down, so there wasn't a lot of choice. The barn had planning permission for conversion to guest accommodation, so I lived in a caravan and did that first, then lived there while I made the house weathertight and sound and installed the basics.'

'So why don't you still live in the cottage? Or let it?'

'Well, I am letting it. I'm letting it to trainees at the moment.'

'But not for as much as you'd get for holiday lets.'

'No, but it's less hassle, and I'm too busy at the weekends to deal with change-overs and guests and their trivial problems and queries. That's the plan, in the end, but not until I've got the house knocked into shape—and with my arms out of action, DIY's taken a definite back seat.'

Lucie chuckled. 'You amaze me. I would have thought you'd have a go anyway.'

He looked rueful. 'I have to confess I did have a go, during the week. I thought I might be able to tackle some of the simple things upstairs, but I couldn't even hold the electric screwdriver with my right hand, and my left—well, let's just say I'm not ambidextrous. Anyway, it still hurts, so what the hell. I gave up.'

And it didn't agree with him, Lucie realised, because he wasn't a quitter.

And nor, she realised with a sinking heart, was Fergus.

They pulled up on the drive beside his car, and Will arched a brow at her. 'Have you got a visitor?'

'Apparently,' she said tightly, and got out of the car at the same time as Fergus emerged from his, a wide smile on his face.

'Lucie, darling! I thought you'd never get here! The dog's been barking its head off—I stayed in the car just in case it got out.'

'You should have rung,' she told him, unable to

be more welcoming, and dredged up a smile. 'I'm sorry we're late. I had evening surgery.'

She offered a cheek for his kiss, and turned to Will, who was coming round the front of the car with a look in his eye that she didn't want to analyse. 'Will, meet Fergus Daly, a friend of mine from London,' she said smoothly. 'Fergus, this is Will Ryan, my trainer.'

'I won't shake hands,' Will said a little curtly, holding up his cast, and looked at Lucie. 'You're obviously busy. If I can have the keys, I'll leave you to it.'

She dropped them in his outstretched hand, and he turned on his heel and strode away, leaving Fergus staring after him.

'What an odd fellow. Not very welcoming.'

Nor was Lucie, but Fergus hadn't noticed—or wasn't acknowledging it. 'So, is this your little *pied-à-terre*?'

She nodded, unlocking the door and pushing it open. 'Come in. I haven't done anything today, it's a bit of a mess. Tea?'

'Nothing stronger?' he said hopefully.

'No, nothing stronger. You're driving.'

'Am I? Where are we going?'

She gave a short sigh. 'To your hotel?'

He reached for her, his hands cupping her shoulders, drawing her towards him. 'I had rather hoped I might be allowed to stay with you,' he murmured, and bent to kiss her.

She turned her head and moved out of his reach. 'I think not, Fergus. I told you that before I left London, and nothing's changed. It was no then, and it's no now.'

'But I miss you, Lucie.'

'I know you miss me—or you think you do—but I don't miss you, Fergus. I'm sorry, but that's the way it is.'

He stood dumbstruck, staring at her with astonished eyes. 'Lucie?'

'Oh, Fergus, come on, it's not as if it's the first time you've heard me say it! We're friends—nothing more. If you can't accept that, then I don't know how else to tell you to make you understand. There is nothing between us—nothing!'

'Oh.' He suddenly seemed to find the carpet absolutely fascinating, and she felt a pang of guilt.

'Fergus, I'm sorry.'

'I was really looking forward to this weekend,' he murmured.

'Only because you've failed to listen to me for weeks now. If you'd been paying attention, you would have realised it was a waste of time.' She moved closer, putting her hand on his arm. 'Have a cup of tea before you go.'

He pulled his arm away and looked up, his eyes suspiciously moist. 'I won't, thank you. I'll get out of your way.' He moved to the door, then paused, looking back at her. 'It's Will, isn't it?'

She sighed. 'No, it's not Will. This was over before I left London, Fergus. Will has nothing to do with it.'

'He may not have been then, but he is now,' he said with unusual perception. 'I hope you find what you're looking for, Lucie. You deserve to, you're a lovely girl.'

The door closed gently behind him, and Lucie sat down and swallowed hard. Poor Fergus. It wasn't his fault he was too safe and too boring. Perhaps it was a failing in her, that she wanted danger and excitement in her relationships?

She looked across at the house, and saw Will standing at the window, watching Fergus drive away, and she wondered what he was thinking.

Then he turned his head and looked towards her, and she felt her heart kick beneath her ribs. Failing or not, it was the way she was, and perhaps this weekend would give her an opportunity to get closer to him. After all, she couldn't rescue him from himself long distance, could she?

A tremor of excitement shivered through her, and she stood up and went into the kitchen area, clearing up her breakfast things and tidying, while her mind plotted her next move.

CHAPTER SEVEN

FERGUS was going off—probably to fetch a take-away or a bottle of fine wine and some candles to romance Lucie. Will was surprised he hadn't brought a hamper with him from Fortnum's. He looked and sounded the type.

The car went up the track away from the house, weaving painstakingly between the potholes, and disappeared from view around the corner of the track. It would probably ground and he'd be back, whimpering about his flashy car that was so tragically unsuited to the rigours of country driving.

He turned away in disgust, and looked at the cottage. Was that Lucie, sitting in the chair on the far side? He couldn't really see, but then she moved, standing up and going into the kitchen, and he wondered what she was doing. Preparing a meal? Setting the scene for the nice romantic dinner Fergus had gone to fetch?

He felt something he didn't really understand and didn't want to analyse, but it burned like a vindaloo. Damn Fergus, with his slick car and polished brogues and slimy manoeuvres. Will didn't know what Fergus had gone to fetch, but he didn't want to hang around and watch the romantic little scene take place.

He called Bruno, put his boots on and stomped down to the river, staying there until it was too cold and too dark for common sense, and then almost had to feel his way back to the house.

There was no sign of Fergus's car, and he thought they'd probably gone out—although he hadn't heard a car. Still, that ostentatious, sexy car wouldn't make a great deal of noise. The engine was the sort that purred rather than growled, and he would certainly take it slowly on the track.

Maybe he *had* grounded it, Will thought, and realised he was gloating. Dammit, that woman was certainly bringing out the worst in him!

He went into the kitchen and put on the kettle, debated lighting the fire and decided he couldn't be bothered. He made some toast, fried a couple of slices of bacon, hacked up a tomato and slapped them together in a sandwich, washing it down with a cup of tea.

He wondered what Lucie and Fergus had had for dinner.

Smoked salmon? Lobster?

Not bacon sandwiches, that was for sure!

There was a knock at the door, and he opened it to find Lucie there, alone.

'Lucie?' he murmured. 'I thought you were out with Fergus.'

She shook her head. 'He's gone,' she said, and he wasn't sure, but he thought she sounded forlorn. Obviously a flying visit that had left her wanting more. Damn.

She looked at the remains of his sandwich clamped in his left hand, then up at his face.

'Is that a bacon sandwich?' she said wistfully, and he gave a crooked smile and opened the door, irrationally pleased to see her and disgustingly glad that Fergus had gone, for whatever reason.

'Want one?'

'I'd kill for one.'

'No need. Just sit patiently at the table and I'll make you one.'

'I'll help.'

So he ended up bumping into her and having her squeeze past him and generally giving his hormones a hard time. She smelt wonderful. He wasn't sure what it was—it might have been shampoo, her hair was still wet from the bath. The thought sent his blood pressure sky-rocketing, and he flipped the bacon onto the toast with an awkward wrist and pushed the plate towards her.

'Here—I'll let you do the tomato, I have to hack it.'

'Forget the tomato, just give me the bacon,' she said with a grin. Picking up the plate, she sat down at the table, one foot hitched up under her bottom, and bit into the sandwich.

Her eyes closed and she groaned with ecstasy, and he had to stifle his own groan of frustration. What *was* it about her?

'This is bliss,' she said with her mouth full. 'I'm starving.'

'Why didn't you eat?'

She shrugged. 'Nothing I fancied in the fridge, and—I don't know, I just didn't feel like it.'

'So you thought you'd come and raid my bacon,' he said, trying hard not to pry and just barely resisting the urge to ask why she hadn't eaten with Fergus.

She laughed self-consciously. 'Actually, I thought I'd see if you were all right. You seemed to be gone for such a long time, and when it got dark I was worried about you.'

'I went down to the river,' he said, a little gruffly

because he was touched at her concern. 'You don't need to worry about me, Lucie, I'm not a kid, you know.'

'I know, but with your arms and everything...'

'Everything?' He smiled. 'You mean my mental disability?'

She grinned. 'You *did* have a head injury.'

He couldn't stop the smile. 'You're crazy,' he said softly, leaning back in the chair and studying her. Her hair was drying in damp tendrils around her face, like a wispy halo, and her mouth was wide and slightly parted and unbelievably sexy. He ached to feel it again under his lips.

'Fancy a coffee?' she suggested. 'It's freezing in here, and I've got the heating on. And Fergus brought me chocolates.'

He'd pass on the chocolates, but only because they'd choke him. Coffee with Lucie in a warm room, though, was too tempting to refuse. He stood up and dumped the plates in the sink. 'Sounds good. What are we waiting for?'

He left Bruno behind, drying off after his frolic in the river, and followed her over to the cottage. She put the kettle on as they went in, then held up a bottle about a third full of something amber and interesting.

'Fancy a malt whisky?' she suggested, and he raised a brow.

'Secret vice?'

She shook her head and smiled. 'My father likes it. He used to pop up to see me from time to time when he was in London on business, and he kept a bottle in my flat. So, do you want some?'

Now he knew it didn't belong to Fergus? 'Just a small one.'

She slopped a hefty measure into a tumbler and handed it to him, and he sat down in one of the wonderfully comfortable armchairs and nursed it while she made the coffee.

It was bliss to sit there with her—not fighting, for once, because he was tired after his walk by the river and the long week and the pain in his arm, and fighting with her would have been too much like hard work.

So he sat, and he sipped his whisky and coffee alternately, and Lucie put some music on softly in the background and curled up opposite him in the other chair, and a great lump of regret formed in his throat that they could never have any more than this.

He sighed softly to himself. What was it about him that made him unable to live with anyone? Every time he'd tried, he'd ended up bitter and resentful. He was just too intolerant, that was the trouble—or maybe nobody had ever been special enough to make the effort for.

Lucie could be special enough, he thought, but they bickered constantly and the irritation he felt was clearly mutual, even if his was largely fueled by sexual frustration.

And anyway, she belonged to Fergus.

'Want a chocolate?' she asked, holding out a box of beautiful hand-made confectionery that must have cost the absent Fergus a small fortune.

He resisted, but Lucie didn't. She tucked in with relish, and he had to watch her sucking and nibbling and fiddling with them—because, of course, being Lucie she couldn't just put one in her mouth and eat it. Oh, no. She had to bite the chocolate off the outside of the hard ones, and curl her tongue inside the soft fondant ones, and generally get totally absorbed in the structure of every single chocolate.

And every bite drove him crazy.

He tried closing his eyes, but that was no better. He imagined her mouth moving over his body, nipping and licking and tormenting the life out of him, and watching her eat the chocolates was probably safer, so he opened them again and found her looking at him, a curious expression on her face.

'What?' he said softly.

'You look as if you're in pain. Is your arm hurting?'

He almost stifled the snort of laughter, but not quite. 'Let's just say I've been more comfortable,' he prevaricated, and crossed one ankle over the other knee to disguise his embarrassment.

She got up to change the CD, and his eyes faithfully tracked the soft curve of her bottom as she bent over the music system. Beautiful. Just lush enough to make the fit of his jeans impossibly tight. Damn. He looked away, into the depths of his malt whisky, and as the slow, sexy music curled round them, he drained the Scotch, stood up and put the glass down with a little smack on the table.

'I have to go.'

'Really?'

She looked wistful, and it occurred to him that she was probably lonely and missing Fergus. He didn't know why the man had left so soon—perhaps it had only ever been meant as a flying visit. Although, thinking about it, she hadn't seemed overjoyed to see him.

'Really,' he said gently. Whatever she was feeling

CAROLINE ANDERSON 125

about Fergus, he didn't want to be used as a substitute.

Liar, his body screamed, but he ignored it until he got to the door, and then he turned to thank her for the coffee and bumped into her, and his hands flew up to cup her shoulders and steady her, and instead of steadying her they drew her closer, just as his head lowered of its own accord and his lips found hers.

She tasted of chocolate and coffee, and her mouth yielded with a tiny sound of surrender that nearly blew his control. Her back was to the bedroom door, and beyond it the bed was only a pace or two away. The knowledge tortured him.

He let go of her shoulders, meaning to ease back, but his arms slid round her of their own volition, drawing her closer, cupping her soft, lush bottom and lifting her into the cradle of his hips.

She gasped softly, and he plundered her mouth, need clawing at him. He wanted her—wanted to hold her and touch her and bury himself deep inside her.

He wanted things he had no business wanting, and she belonged to Fergus.

With a deep groan he released her, stepping back and fumbling behind him for the doorhandle. 'Lucie, I...' He trailed off, lost for words, and she put a finger over his lips.

'Shh. Don't say anything.'

He took her hand, lifting it slightly and pressing a lingering kiss into the palm. 'I have to go.'

'I know. I'll see you tomorrow.'

She came up on tiptoe and kissed his cheek, her soft breasts bumping into his chest and tormenting him again. He pulled the door open and backed through it, almost falling over the cat.

'Damn, she's sneaked in,' he said, but Lucie laughed, a low, sexy little laugh that tortured him.

'She always sneaks in. I don't mind. She comes through the bedroom window most nights and sleeps on the bed.'

Lucky cat, he thought enviously, and dredged up a crooked, rather tragic smile. 'See you tomorrow.'

He turned and strode back to his house, refusing to allow himself to look back over his shoulder, and let himself in. Bruno greeted him with a thump of his tail, and he patted the dog absently and went upstairs to bed.

There was no way he would sleep, but his body was tired and he needed to rest.

Correction. He needed Lucie, and he wasn't about to get her.

Not now, not ever.

Lucie went to bed, her lips still tingling from his kiss. Poor Fergus. He was right. Will hadn't been an issue before she'd left London, but he certainly was now, and even if Fergus had been in with a chance before, that would have changed.

Especially after Will's kiss.

Fergus had kissed her before, of course, but only fairly briefly, because it had been all she'd allowed. She would have given Will anything he'd asked for.

Anything.

She reached for her diary, and wrote, 'Progress. We kissed again. He still seemed to regret it, but I don't. Oh, no! Wish he could have stayed the night.'

She put the diary down and switched off the light, then curled up on her side and relived the kiss. It brought an ache that wouldn't go away, an ache that was more than just physical and gave her a lump in her throat, because some time in the course of that kiss, she'd realised that she loved him.

How could she possibly have fallen in love with someone so grumpy and touchy and difficult?

Because that isn't the real him? her alter ego suggested. Because the real him is gentle and tender and loving, and crying out for a partner to share life's trials?

Crying out for peace and quiet and solitude, more like, she corrected herself. She didn't think for a moment that Will was looking for a partner. A more solitary person she didn't think she'd ever met, and even now, wanting her as he very obviously did, he still resented it.

Why?

Maybe Richard would know, but it seemed a little unfair to ask his senior partner to tell her about Will's personal life. She wouldn't want it done to her.

So, then, she'd have to ask him directly.

Or not!

Will rapped on Lucie's door at ten-thirty, just as she finished clearing up after her breakfast. She wiped her hands on her jeans and opened the door, greeting him with a smile that probably said far too much. She'd never been good at keeping her feelings secret.

'Hi, come in,' she said cheerfully. 'Coffee?'

'I get a definite feeling of *déjà vu*,' he murmured, and she swallowed hard. Heavens, he looked sexy today! He was wearing jeans, the same snug-fitting jeans he'd been wearing when he'd fallen, if she remembered correctly, so his fingers must be better with buttons now.

'Is that a yes or a no?' she asked, going to put the kettle on anyway.

'Make it a yes,' he said, following her. 'I've been thinking—about your training.'

Her heart sank. Oh, no, she thought, he's going to say he can't go on doing it because of our personal involvement and I'm going to have to go away.

'The patients are all being too obliging,' he continued. 'Apart from Harriet with her hairball and Mr Gregory with his gastric problems, they're all too cut and dried, and none of them are being awkward. You aren't getting enough experience with the awkward ones.'

She laughed and turned to face him, astonished. 'So what are you asking me to do? Argue with them? Tell them they're boring?'

'Role play,' he said, and her jaw dropped.

'Role play?' she parroted weakly. Of all the things she'd hated about her entire education, role play was top of the list. Oh, she was good at it—but she couldn't seem to take it seriously, and she always wanted to add something trivial to mess it up.

She'd been in constant trouble with the drama teacher at school, and her clinical medicine tutors had thrown up their hands in despair at her attitude.

And now Will, who already thought she was a silly, flighty little piece, wanted her to do role-play exercises *with him*?

'I can't do it,' she said firmly.

'Yes, you can,' he told her, just as firmly. 'You just have to try. You'll feel self-conscious for a while, but then you'll get used to it.'

Self-conscious? Not a chance! She'd probably just shock him so badly she'd fail this part of her training.

Still, he had that implacable look on his face, and she had a feeling he intended to win this argument.

'When?' she said, resigning herself to disaster.

'Now?'

'Now!' She nearly dropped the coffee. 'Now, as in *now*?'

He shrugged. 'Are you busy? We can always do it another time.'

'But it's your weekend,' she said feebly, hunting for excuses.

He raised his hands, one in a cast, the other still swollen and in a support. 'And there's so much else I can do.'

You could make love to me, she thought, and for a moment she wondered if she'd said it out loud. Apparently not, because he calmly took the coffee she passed him and set it down without incident on the table beside him.

'I don't bite,' he said softly, and she stifled a laugh.

'OK,' she agreed, giving in. It might be a bit of fun, and if she didn't overdo it, maybe he wouldn't get too mad with her.

He knocked on the door, and she opened it and drew him in. 'Hello, there,' she said brightly. 'I'm Dr Compton—come in and sit down. What can I do for you?'

Wouldn't you like to know? Will thought, and limped over to the chair. 'I'm having trouble with my bowels, Doctor,' he said, and met her eyes.

They were sparkling with mischief, and he sighed inwardly. She'd make a lousy poker player. 'What sort of trouble?' she asked.

'Oh, you know—either I go or I don't.'

Her lips twitched. 'How long's it been going on?' she said. 'Is it a recent problem, or have you always been like this, or does it come and go?'

'Oh, comes and goes,' he ad libbed. 'Well, it has done recently. Never used to. I used to have it all the time.'

'And what exactly is the trouble?' she probed.

'Well, as I say, either I go, or—I don't.'

'Have you changed your diet?'

'Well, not really. Stopped eating vegetables after my Katie died.'

'Oh, I see. So your wife died recently?'

'Oh, no, not my wife. Katie was the dog.'

Her mouth twitched, and Will had to admit he was having trouble keeping a straight face. However, she carried on. 'So, are you still eating less vegetables?'

'I get meals on wheels. I don't like soggy sprouts. Every day it's soggy sprouts—either that or cabbage, or those awful tinned carrots. You ever had those tinned carrots, Doctor?'

'Not that I recall. So, you're probably not eating enough vegetables. How about fruit?'

'I like tinned peaches,' he said, wondering how long he could keep her going. 'Strawberries, though—they're my favourite, although they usually give me the trouble.'

'You mean, you go?'

'Oh, yes. Well, of course, it depends how many I have. If I have too many, then I do, but if I don't have too many, I—'

'Don't,' she said with him, meeting his eyes in a direct challenge. 'I see. So how about apples, pears, that sort of thing? Breakfast cereal?'

'You're talking about roughage, aren't you, Doctor? Never had no shortage of that in the war. I remember—'

'And you were all probably a lot healthier for it,' she said, cutting him off neatly before he had time to ramble. 'Still, we need to worry about what would help you now, and see what we can do to make things more regular.'

'Oh, yes, regular, that's what I'd like to be,' he said fervently, stifling the smile. Her eyes twinkled. He should have been warned, but he wasn't, and her next remark shocked him.

'I think I need to examine you,' she said blandly. 'If you could slip your trousers down and lie on the couch.' She pointed at the settee, and he raised an eyebrow. 'Please?' she added.

'Is this really necessary?' he asked in his usual voice.

She propped her hands her hips and looked at him with that sassy little smile, all innocent and wicked at once. 'Of course. How will you know if I've been sufficiently thorough if I don't do everything I would normally do?'

'Hmm,' he muttered under his breath. 'We'll imagine the trousers,' he said firmly, and lay down, his legs dangling over the end.

'I'll just undo them,' she said, and before he could protest the button fly was popping open and her little hands were in there, prodding and poking about at his innards and getting perilously close to finding out just how much he was getting out of this whole bit of nonsense.

She tugged up his shirt and peered at the skin of

his abdomen. 'Nice neat scar—is that appendix or a hernia repair?' she asked innocently.

'Appendix,' he said in a strangled voice.

'And have you had trouble ever since it was removed?'

Damn, how did she keep it going? 'Well, off and on. Like I said, sometimes I go, and—'

'Sometimes you don't. Yes. I remember.' She pressed down in the centre of his abdomen and released sharply, and he obligingly grunted, feigning rebound tenderness.

'Oh, dear, was that a bit sore?' she asked sympathetically.

'It was.'

Mischief danced in her eyes. 'What about if I do it here, further down?'

He caught her wrists, just in the nick of time. 'I think we get the picture,' he said, swinging his legs off the settee and struggling to fasten his jeans.

'Here, let me,' she said, and then those little fingers were in there again, brushing against his abdomen and driving him crazy. He sucked in his breath to get out of her way, but she was done, and he tugged the rest of the shirt out of the waistband and let it provide a little modesty.

Had she noticed? Goodness knows, but he wasn't taking any chances. He sat back down in his chair and crossed his leg over his other knee. He seemed to spend a lot of time in this position, he thought, and sighed.

Perhaps role play wasn't such a good idea after all.

* * *

Lucie was enjoying herself. They swapped roles, they touched on difficult and serious issues, and other more trivial and silly ones, and she did learn a lot from him.

She also learned a lot about him. She learned that he had a sense of humour—a wonderful sense of humour, every bit as wicked as her own—and that he cared deeply about his patients, and that he was a stickler for exactitude and wouldn't tolerate inconsistencies.

If she was vague he chivvied her up, making her be more specific, and although she threw in the odd bit of nonsense to liven the proceedings, in fact it was astonishingly easy to get into the roles with him and she found herself doing it seriously.

She also learned that she could turn him on just by stroking her fingers over the tender skin of his abdomen, so that his body betrayed his true reactions despite the fact that he stayed in role.

And she learned that as far as he was concerned, that was a no-go area and she wasn't to be allowed to tease him into breaking out of role.

Finally, at about lunchtime, he sat back and blew out his breath in a long stream. 'Well?'

'Thank you,' she said, genuinely meaning it. 'That was very useful. How did I do?'

'When you were being serious? Fine. Very good, mostly. The rest is just experience, but I think you've got what it takes. I think you'll do, Lucie Compton. If you were my GP, I'd be confident I was being looked after properly.'

Her cheeks coloured softly, and she let out a soft laugh. 'Well—thanks, Dr Ryan.'

'My pleasure. I think we deserve lunch. How about going to the pub?'

She wrinkled her nose. 'Typical. I'm driving, of course.'

He grinned. 'That's right, but fair's fair. As you so rightly pointed out, I just gave up my Saturday morning for you, so I deserve a drink more than you.'

There was no answer to that.

CHAPTER EIGHT

WITH her confidence bolstered by Will's praise, Lucie found working with him easier after that, although he continued to make notes and criticise and nit-pick.

Still, his comments were all fair and helpful and, although it annoyed her, she could see the point.

A fortnight after their role-play session, Harriet Webb came to see her for a check-up. She'd been discharged from hospital a week earlier, and before they arranged to go on holiday at the end of May, her mother wanted to be sure she would be well enough. Lucie had to admit Harriet looked considerably better than she had when they'd first seen her.

Her hair was cut short, as well—spiky and fun and a very pretty style that was too short to pull out in her sleep.

'Are you finding it easier to eat now?' Lucie asked her, and Harriet laughed.

'I'm starving. I've never been so hungry in my life. I think it's having room to really eat—I've probably never had that before. They said the hairball has probably been forming all my life. It was amazing— they showed it to me, and it was just the shape of my stomach and so huge! All my clothes are loose now, and my waist is so much smaller. They're putting it in their museum at the hospital, for the nurse training department, so I'll be famous. How cool is that?'

Lucie chuckled. 'Ultra-cool. You look good. I like the hair.'

She patted it experimentally. 'I'm still getting used to it. I used to fiddle with it all the time. It's like having my hands cut off! Still, I don't want another of those things, no way!' She shuddered.

'Are you seeing anyone about why you might have done it?' Lucie asked cautiously, and Harriet pulled a face.

'You mean the therapist? She's useless.'

'Give her a chance,' Lucie urged. 'She might be able to help you find out why you did it, and I know it might not be what you want to do, rummaging around inside all your personal thoughts and feelings, but if it stops it happening again and helps you move forward, that has to be good, doesn't it?'

Harriet nodded. 'I s'pose. It's just all a bit—I don't know. She keeps going back to when I was little and my sister died, and it—you know. It's difficult to talk about. I don't like to remember.'

'I'm sure,' Lucie said with sympathy.

Mrs Webb was sitting quietly in the background, and she met Lucie's eyes and shrugged helplessly. 'She seemed all right at the time, although it was awful, but that's when the hair thing started. Maybe this girl can get to the bottom of her problems. We're hopeful.'

'Well, as far as I'm concerned she's in excellent physical shape now and I can't see any reason why you shouldn't go on holiday. I expect it will do you all good. Are you going anywhere nice?'

'Only France,' Mrs Webb said. 'We go most years, but we thought we'd go earlier this year, to give Harriet a treat.'

'Well, I hope you have a lovely time,' Lucie said with a smile as they left.

'Make a note of that,' Will said from behind her.

'Of the sister?'

'Yes. Sounds as if Harriet was involved in some way in her death—maybe she found her, or feels it was her fault. Whatever, it could be relevant. Just jot it down.'

'I have.' She turned to face him. 'She's looking better, isn't she? Funny hangover, that.'

Will smiled slightly, letting her score the point. 'Who's next?' he asked.

'Mr Gregory. He's had the course of treatment for his *H. pylori*—this is a follow-up. Hopefully he's better.'

He was. He felt better than he had for months, he said, and although the treatment had been awful, it had done the trick and he felt much more like his old self.

'So, how's the diet going now?' Lucie asked. 'Dr Ryan tells me you're trying to cut down and lose a few kilos.'

'Oh, well, I gave all that up when this got out of hand, but I suppose I could start again. Maybe I need a bit less dressing on the salad. That seemed to set me off.'

'You don't have to eat salad just because you're on a diet,' Lucie reminded him. 'You can have normal meals, but cooked with much less fat, and with low-fat gravy and sauces and loads of veg. It doesn't have to be cold and raw to be less fattening!'

He chuckled. 'I know. Somehow it feels more like a diet, though, if it's cold. Still, I'll persevere.'

'Why don't we weigh you now, since you're here,

and we can check you again in a few weeks? Slip off your jacket and shoes, that's right.'

She weighed him, jotted it down on his notes and smiled. 'Well, I'm glad the treatment worked.'

'So am I. I'll go and have some hot tomatoes.'

He went out chuckling, and Will rolled his eyes. 'The nurse can weigh him.'

'He was in here.'

'And your next patient should have been. You're running behind now.'

She turned to face him again. 'Are you sure you aren't well enough to go and do something useful, like run a surgery?'

'With only one hand? Hardly. I've told you, I'm hopeless with my left hand. How could I do internals?'

'You couldn't. You'd have to ask for help.'

'And if there was nobody about? Don't worry, Lucie, I've thought about it. This is working.'

Not for me, she wanted to say, but that wasn't fair. They only crossed swords a few times a day now, instead of a few times an hour.

Progress?

The phone rang, and she picked it up. 'Dr Compton.'

'Doctor, I've got Mrs Brown on the line. She's expecting triplets? She says she's got cramp in her stomach and she's a bit worried. Could you go?'

She covered the receiver and repeated the message to Will. 'I'll talk to her,' he said, and took the phone.

After a brief exchange, he said, 'All right, hang on, we'll come now. You stay where you are.'

'I have a surgery.'

'The patients can either wait or switch to Richard,'

he said firmly. 'Angela Brown is about to lose her triplets, unless I'm very much mistaken, and I want to see her now. She can't wait. They can.' He nodded towards the waiting room.

'OK. I'll get my bag.'

'Come on, Lucie, move. She's in distress.'

They moved. They got there within ten minutes, to find that Angela had started to bleed.

It was only a little trickle, but her blood pressure was low and it was likely that she was haemorrhaging.

'I think you need the obstetric flying squad,' he told her gently. 'I'm sorry, but you need to be in hospital now, and you need a qualified obstetric team with you.'

'What about the babies?' she asked worriedly.

'I don't know about the babies. At the moment I'm worried about you. Lucie, can you call?' He told her the number, and she rang, relayed his instructions and asked for immediate assistance while he checked Angela's blood pressure again and listened to the babies through the foetal stethoscope.

'She needs a line in,' he instructed, and Lucie put an intravenous connector into her hand, ready for the drip, and took some blood for cross-matching, just in case.

'Shouldn't you examine me?' Angela asked them, and Will shook his head.

'No. You don't want to be poked about—it can cause the uterus to contract, and it might settle down. I want you in hospital fast, and I want that specialist team with you, just to be on the safe side. And in the meantime, I want you to lie as still as you can and not worry.'

It seemed to take ages for the obstetric team to arrive, but when it did, they moved smoothly into action and Will and Lucie shut up the house and followed them out.

'I wonder if she'll lose them?' Lucie said thoughtfully. 'She was so worried about having them, and now she's worried about not having them.'

'I don't know. Maybe they'll live, maybe not. Whatever, it'll be hard for her. I have to say my instinct is she'd be better without them, but I doubt if she'd see that in the same way as me.'

Lucie doubted it, too, and was glad she didn't have to make those sorts of choices. Nature would take its course, aided and abetted—or thwarted, depending on how you looked at it—by medical intervention, and Mrs Brown would come out at the end somehow, unless there was a drastic hiccup.

They went back to the surgery to find that Richard had finished her patients for her and everyone was in the office, sipping champagne.

'What are we celebrating?' Will asked, and Gina, one of the receptionists, waved her hand at them.

'Look! He finally did it!'

Will grabbed her flailing hand and peered at the ring, then gave her a hug. 'Congratulations. He took some pinning down.'

'Absolutely. Still, it's all going ahead now, and because I don't trust him not to change his mind, it's on Friday afternoon. Now, I know you can't skive off, all of you, but you can come to a party in the evening, can't you?'

'I'm sure we can all manage that, can't we?' Richard agreed, and fixed Will with a look. 'And since Will's broken his arm and won't be up a ladder, I imagine you'll even get him.'

'And Lucie—if you'd like to,' Gina said with a beaming smile. Lucie guessed that just then she'd have invited all the patients as well if there had been any about, but Lucie agreed, as much as anything because she thought it might be interesting to see Will at a party.

And who knows? she thought. It might even be fun.

'I really, really don't want to go,' Will said with a sigh.

Lucie looked at him across the car. 'You have to, Will. You said you would, and it's her wedding day.'

He sighed again. 'I know. I'm going. I just don't want to.'

'It might be fun,' she said encouragingly, and he shot her a black look.

'That's exactly what I'm afraid of,' he said darkly.

'Oh, pooh. You need to lighten up,' she said with grin. 'You never know, we might get you doing Karaoke by the end of the evening.'

'Hmm. See that pig up there in the sky?'

She chuckled, and opened the door. 'Come on. We have to get ready. We've got to leave in an hour. Do you want me to put your glove on?'

'Please,' he agreed, so she went in with him, waited while he stripped off his shirt and helped him into the long loose glove he'd got off a veterinary friend. A rubber band around the top held it in place, and it covered the entire cast without messing around with tape.

And that, they were both agreed, was a huge improvement.

The only problem was that she had to put it on after he'd taken off his shirt, and so she was treated on an almost daily basis to the delicious sight of Will's muscular and enviable torso, just inches away.

Close enough to touch.

She snapped the elastic band in place, flashed him a grin and all but ran back to her cottage. He could get the glove off, so her time was now her own, and she had to bath, wash her hair and get it into some semblance of order, and put her glad rags on.

The party was in a village hall, and she didn't think it would be dreadfully smart, but it might be quite dressy in a different sort of way, and she sifted through her clothes until she found black trousers and a flirty, floaty top with a camisole under it that dressed the whole thing up.

She put on her make-up, added a bit more jewellery and stood back and looked at herself. Fine. A little brash, but what the hell? She wasn't going out to one of Fergus's posh restaurants, she was going to a wedding party in a village hall, and she intended to have fun.

Lucie didn't know what she was doing to him. She was like a bright little butterfly, flitting about in that gauzy bit of nonsense. Granted, she wore a little top under it, but even so!

And she was in her element, of course. She could talk to anyone, and she did. She talked to everyone, without exception, from the bride's father to the kids in the corner who were throwing peanuts at the guests and giggling.

She threw one at him and it landed in his drink, splashing him. He met her eyes, and she was laughing, her hand over her mouth, looking as guilty as the kids and as full of mischief.

He shook his head in despair and turned back to his conversation with Richard's wife. She, however, seemed quite happy to be distracted by Lucie.

'What a charming girl,' she said, and Will nearly groaned.

'Yes, she is. Well, she can be.'

'And you can be charming, too, of course, if you put your mind to it,' Sylvia said in gentle reprimand.

'Sorry.' He gave her a rueful smile. 'I'm just feeling a bit old.'

'Old?' She laughed. 'You wait until you hit forty-five, if you want to feel old! Did Richard tell you we're going to be grandparents?'

'No, he didn't. Congratulations.'

She pulled a face. 'I'm pleased really, I suppose, but I had hoped they'd wait until they were a bit more secure.'

'What, like you did?'

She laughed and slapped his arm, her hand bouncing harmlessly off the cast. 'You know what I mean.'

'Yes, I do. But there's a danger to that, you know, Sylvia. You can be too measured, too organised, too planned. And then you find that life's gone on without you.'

'Well, this party's certainly going on without you,' she admonished, standing up. 'Come on, you can dance with me.'

'What?'

'Come on, you can't refuse, it's rude.' She pulled him to his feet and dragged him to the dance floor, and he could feel Lucie's eyes on his back all the way across the room.

Sylvia was kind to him and let him shuffle without expecting anything too outrageous.

And then the music changed, and Lucie appeared at their sides.

'I believe this is the ladies' excuse-me,' she said with a smile to Sylvia, and slid neatly into Will's arms before he could protest.

The cast felt awkward against her back, but his fingertips could feel the subtle shift of her spine, and he cradled her right hand in his left against his chest, his thumb idly tracing the back of her fingers. Her breast chafed against the back of his hand, and he could feel the occasional brush of her thighs against his.

It felt good. Too good, really, but he wasn't stopping. It was a genuine reason to hold her, and he was going to make the best of it!

And then the best man commandeered the microphone, and announced that the Karaoke machine was now working and they wanted the bride and groom to kick off.

'I'm out of here,' Will muttered, and Lucie laughed and led him back to their table.

'It'll be a laugh. Just go with the flow.'

So he did, and, in fact, it wasn't as awful as he'd imagined. Lots of the guests had a go, and some of them were quite good, and everyone seemed to enjoy themselves. Then, to his horror and amazement, Lucie was pounced on.

'Come on, you can sing, we've heard you,' the receptionists told her, and Will watched, transfixed, as she was towed, laughing, to the stage and presented with the microphone by the best man.

'So, ladies and gentlemen, here we go. It's Dr Lucie Compton singing Whitney Houston's song from *The Bodyguard*, "And I Will Always Love You". Let's hear it for Lucie!'

The crowd clapped and cheered, and then went quiet for the slow, haunting introduction. Lord, she was wonderful! Will felt his skin shiver, and then as she reached the first repeat of the title, her eyes found his, and he felt a huge lump in his throat.

There was no way she was singing it for him, but he could let himself dream, and then she hit the volume and he went cold all over with the power of her voice.

Lord, she was spectacular! He'd had no idea she was *so* good, and neither, by the look of them, had any of the others. She was really into it now, her voice mellow and yet pure, every note true, every word filled with meaning.

She finished, holding the last note until Will thought she'd die of lack of oxygen, but then she cut it and bowed, laughing, as the guests went wild.

'Encore!' 'Again!' 'More!' they yelled, and she turned to the best man and shrugged.

'OK. What have you got?'

'What can you do?'

She laughed. 'Anything. Try me.'

He did, and she was right. She knew them all, and hardly fluffed a note. Most of the time she didn't even glance at the monitor for the words, and Will was stunned. Finally, though, she surrendered the microphone to thunderous applause, and came back to the table.

'Sorry about that, I got hijacked,' she said with a chuckle, and pointed to his drink. 'Is that just mineral water?'

'Yes.'

'May I?'

He pushed it towards her, and she drained it, then set it down with a grin.

'I enjoyed that. I haven't done it for ages.'

'You were good,' he said gruffly. 'Very good.' Stunning.

She smiled a little shyly. 'Thanks,' she said, as if she really cared what he thought, and he wanted to hug her. Well, he wanted to do more than hug her, but it would be a good start.

'So how come you know them all?' he asked, trying to concentrate on something other than holding her in his arms, and she shrugged.

'I used to sing in a nightclub to earn money when I was at college,' she explained. 'The hours fitted, and the money was good, and I enjoyed it mostly, except for the smoke and the lechers.'

Will was feeling pretty much of a lecher himself just now, but he didn't want to think too much about that.

'I could kill a drink,' Lucie said, and he thought for a moment he was going to have to walk across the room in his state of heightened awareness, but he was saved by the best man descending on them and buying them both drinks to thank Lucie for her contribution to the evening.

The Karaoke had packed up after she'd sung. She was, as they said, a hard act to follow, and so they'd gone back to the disco music and everyone was dancing again.

They had a drink, and this time Will had a whisky. Well, he wasn't driving, and he needed something to act as anaesthetic if he was going to sleep that night!

'Are you ready to go?' he asked her a short while later, and she grinned and stuck her finger under his chin, tickling it.

'Is it past your bedtime, you poor old thing?' she crooned, and he nearly choked.

Way past, he thought, but not in the way she was implying! He glowered at her, and she just laughed and stood up. 'Come on, then, Cinderella, your carriage awaits.'

They said goodbye to their hosts, and twenty minutes later they were pulling up outside the house and she was going to go her way and he was going to have to go his, and he suddenly didn't want the evening to end.

God, however, was on his side. 'Coffee?' she said, and he sent up a silent word of thanks.

'That would be lovely.'

He followed her into the cottage and stood leaning on the old timber-stud wall in the kitchen while she put the kettle on. 'So, did you have fun?' she asked him, turning to face him and standing with one hand on her hip in an unconsciously provocative pose.

His libido leapt to life again. 'Yes, I had fun,' he confessed. 'You were wonderful, Lucie. You've got a beautiful voice.'

'Thanks.'

She met his eyes again, that shy smile playing over her lips, and he suddenly knew he'd die if he didn't kiss her.

He hadn't kissed her for weeks—three weeks, to

be exact, not since Fergus had been down, and it had
been far too long.

He held out his arms, and she moved into them
without a murmur, pressing her body softly up
against him as she turned her face up for his kiss.

A deep groan dragged itself up from the depths of
his body, and his mouth found hers and relief poured
through him.

Not for long, though. He shifted against her, ach-
ing for her, and with a tiny moan she pressed herself
harder against him and wrapped her arms around his
neck. Her fingers tunnelled through his hair, her body
wriggled against him and then finally she lifted her
head, undid the top buttons of his shirt and laid her
lips against his skin.

Heat exploded in him, and he gave a deep groan.
'Lucie, in the name of God, what are you doing?' he
asked in a strangled voice, and she laughed a little
unsteadily.

'You need lessons?' she said, and her voice was
deep and husky and unbelievably sexy.

'I don't need lessons. I thought I was the trainer.'

'Mmm,' she murmured, nuzzling the base of his
throat. 'You are. How am I doing?'

'Just fine,' he croaked, and, putting his fingers under her chin, he tilted her face firmly up to face him.
'Don't tease me, Lucie.'

Her eyes lost their playful look and became in-
tensely serious. 'I'm not teasing,' she vowed. 'I want
to make love with you.'

Will closed his eyes and let his breath out in a
rush. She wanted to make love with him, and had he
thought of this in advance? Was he prepared?

He felt as if he'd won the lottery and lost the ticket.

'We can't,' he said. 'No protection.'

'Yes, we have,' Lucie said, and smiled a smile as old as time.

It had lost nothing of its power over the countless generations. He felt as if his knees were going to buckle, and when she moved away and held out her hand, he took it and followed her through to the bedroom.

She was incredible. She was gentle, teasing, earnest—she was a thousand different women, and he wanted them all. He wanted her, and he could think of nothing else.

It was only afterwards, when he lay spent beside her, his heart pounding and his body exhausted, that he remembered that she belonged to Fergus...

CHAPTER NINE

LUCIE woke to a feeling of utter contentment. She'd never—*never*—been loved like that, and she felt whole as she'd never felt whole in her life before.

She opened her eyes, a smile forming on her lips, but Will was gone. She sat up, throwing off the quilt, not heeding her nakedness. 'Will?'

There was no reply, and the cottage was too quiet. Quiet with the silence of emptiness. She felt ice slide over her and, shivering, she pulled on her dressing-gown and went through to the sitting room. She knew he wasn't in the bathroom, because the door had been open and there was no sign of him.

Nor was he in the sitting room. She felt the kettle, and it was stone cold. When had he left? Just now, or earlier in the night?

She looked across at his house, but it was daylight and there would be no lights on anyway. She went back into the bedroom and felt the other side of the bed but, like the kettle, it was cold. He must have gone back to let the dog out, she realised, and stayed.

He was bound to be up, though, so she showered quickly, threw on her jeans and an old rugby shirt and some thick socks, and went over to the house. The back door was open, as usual, and she went in and found him sitting at the table, staring broodingly into a mug.

'Hi,' she said softly.

Will looked up, and to her surprise his eyes were

unreadable. They certainly hadn't been unreadable last night, but today they were. Distant and remote and expressionless. 'Hi.'

She faltered, suddenly uncertain of her welcome and not knowing why. 'Is something wrong?' she asked with her usual directness, and he shrugged.

'I don't do the morning-after thing very well.'

She stared at him. 'I noticed,' she said wryly, and went over to the kettle. 'Mind if I have a cup of tea?'

'Help yourself. You usually do.'

Oh, lord. All that beautiful intimacy, the tenderness, the whispered endearments—all gone, wiped out with the dawn. She felt sick inside, cold and afraid.

'Have you had breakfast?' she asked, striving for normality, and he shook his head.

'Not yet.'

'Want some toast?'

'If you're making it.'

Well, he wasn't going to make it easy, that was for sure, but she wasn't giving up either.

She cut four slices of bread, stuck them in the toaster and sat down opposite him, so he couldn't avoid looking at her.

He did, though. He stared down into his tea as if his life depended on it, and when she reached out a hand and touched him, he all but recoiled.

'Have I done something wrong?' she asked gently.

He looked up then, his eyes piercing and remote. 'No. Ignore me. I'm always like this.'

'Might explain why you're still single at thirty-three, then,' she said lightly, and went to collect the toast.

They ate in silence, and when he'd finished he

scraped his chair back and stood up. 'I'm taking the dog out.'

'Mind if I come?'

He shrugged. 'Please yourself. You usually do, but I'm going down by the river and your trainers will get ruined.'

'I've got boots. Give me a minute.'

She ran over to the cottage, dug out the wellies that hadn't seen the light of day for years and pulled them on, snagged a jacket off the hook by the door and went back out to find Will standing on the edge of the track, his hands rammed in his pockets, Bruno running in circles round the lawn barking impatiently.

As soon as he saw her, he turned and headed off, not waiting for her to catch up, and feeling sick inside she hurried after him, drawing level just in time to fall behind as the path narrowed.

And he wasn't hanging around for her or making any concessions, of course. Oh, no. That would be out of character. Whoever had made such beautiful love to her last night had been put firmly back in his place and the Will she knew—and loved?—was back with a vengeance.

She struggled down the path after him over the uneven ground, and finally, when she thought she'd die of exhaustion, they arrived at the river. Thank God, she thought, but that wasn't the end of it.

He turned sharply left and carried on along the path, striding out so that she almost had to run to catch up. Well, damn him, she wouldn't run! She slowed down, taking her time to enjoy the walk, looking out over the quiet beauty of the morning light on the water, and she thought she'd never seen anything quite so lovely in her life.

They were near the sea, and gulls were wheeling overhead, their keening cry reminding her of seaside holidays as a child. A wader was standing on one leg, and the water was so still she could see the ripples spreading out in the water around it, perfectly concentric rings interrupted only by the thin stalks of the reeds that broke the surface of the water in places.

It stabbed the mud with its beak, breaking the pattern, and she breathed again and moved on, following Will and wondering how anyone who loved this land as he so obviously did could be so changeable.

Maybe he loved it because it, too, constantly changed, continually affected by external influences.

Or was Will just bad-tempered and grumpy, and was she making too many allowances for him?

Probably, she acknowledged, looking ahead to where he was standing waiting for her, staring out over the river, his body utterly motionless.

Then he turned his head, and she told herself she imagined the pain in his eyes. Over that distance she could hardly make out his features, never mind read an expression!

Lucie hurried towards him, and this time he waited until she reached him.

'It's beautiful,' she said softly, and he nodded.

'I try and come down here every day. It's harder in the winter because it's dark so early, but I still try. Sometimes it freezes, and the birds skid about on the ice at the sides and Bruno tries to chase them. He always falls through, though. It never freezes that hard.'

She smiled, imagining it, and looked up at him.

His eyes tracked over her face, and she reached up and laid her hand on his cheek. 'You haven't kissed me this morning,' she said, and, going up on tiptoe, she brushed his lips with hers.

'Lucie,' he whispered, and then his arms went round her and his mouth found hers again and he kissed with a trembling hesitation that brought tears to her eyes.

Then Will lifted his head and stared out over the river again, and this time she saw the pain quite clearly, for the second it took him to gather his composure around him like a cloak.

'We shouldn't have made love last night,' he said, and his voice sounded rusty, as if he'd left it down by the river at the water's edge for the tide to wash over it and reclaim it.

Her knees threatened to buckle. Why? she wanted to cry, but she couldn't speak. Her throat had closed, clogged with tears, and it was as much as she could do to breathe.

She turned away before he could see the tears in her eyes, and headed back up to the house. She was damned if she'd let him see her cry!

She heard the drumming of hoofbeats, and in the distance she could make out Amanda and Henry, flying along the track that ran along the far side of the field beside her.

She felt a pang of envy. To feel the wind in your face and see the trees rushing past and feel so free— it must be wonderful. She brushed aside the tears and turned her attention back to the path, concentrating on putting one foot in front of the other.

And then she heard the unearthly scream, and the

hideous crash, and, looking up, she saw Henry struggling to his feet, unable to stand properly.

'Oh, my God,' she whispered. 'Oh, Amanda!'

She turned her head to call Will, but he'd seen and
heard as well, and he was running up the field towards them, his long legs eating up the ground,
Bruno streaking ahead.

She ran after him, her breath tearing in her throat,
and adrenaline was surging through her, making her
heart pound so hard she thought it would come out
of her chest.

Will had reached Amanda now, and he was kneel-
ing down when Lucie ran up, and his face was ashen.

'I think she's dead,' he said, and his voice was
hollow and empty.

Lucie dropped to her knees beside him. 'She can't
be. Let me feel.'

'She's not breathing, and I can't feel a pulse. I
think her neck's broken, but I can't do anything with
this bloody stupid hand...'

Lucie slipped her fingers behind the back of
Amanda's neck, but she could feel nothing displaced.
'Maybe not. She might just be winded. Run and get
my bag, and call an ambulance. You can go faster
than me, and I've got hands that work. Take the dog
with you.'

He was gone before she'd finished speaking, and
she quickly ran her fingers down under Amanda's
spine, feeling for any irregularity. If there was one,
it was undetectable. So why...?

'Come on, Amanda, you can't do this,' she said.
Ripping open her shirt, she laid her head on
Amanda's chest. Yes, there was a faint heartbeat, but
she wasn't breathing. Her airway, Lucie thought,

and, supporting the neck by sliding her hand under it, she lifted Amanda's chin.

Amanda gasped, and as Lucie continued to support her neck, her eyelids fluttered open and she dragged in another breath.

Lucie let hers out in a rush. 'You're all right. Just lie still, you'll be OK.'

'Hurt,' she whispered.

'I know. Lie still, Will's getting the ambulance. Where do you hurt?'

'Everywhere. Legs—back—don't know. Pelvis?'

Lucie nodded. Amanda's legs were lying at a very strange angle, and it was obvious that she was very seriously injured. The first thing she needed was a neck brace, just to be on the safe side.

'You'll be OK,' she told her without any great faith, and prayed for Will to hurry. She wanted to get a line in, so that the ambulance crew could get some fluids into her as soon as possible to counteract the shock, because Lucie could tell that Amanda's blood pressure was going down, and goodness knows what internal injuries she might have sustained.

'Henry,' Amanda whispered a little breathlessly. 'Is he...?'

'He's over there, behind you. He's up.' On three legs, with the fourth dangling at a very strange angle, but Amanda didn't need to know that. 'Do you know what happened?'

'No. He—just seemed to—hit something—in the grass. Don't know what. Is he all right?'

'I don't know anything about horses,' Lucie said with perfect truth. 'Just keep very still, sweetheart. Try not to move.'

Amanda's eyes fluttered shut then, and Lucie had

never felt more alone in her life. Come on, Will, she thought, and then he appeared, her medical bag in his left hand, a bundle of towels and sheets under his right arm.

'Any joy?'

'She's breathing. Her airway was obstructed. I think her tongue had been driven back with the force of the fall. She's just resting.'

He looked down at her, just as Amanda's eyes opened and she looked up at him. 'Will? Look after Henry.'

'I will.'

'Got insurance. Call the vet. Anything…'

'OK. Don't worry about Henry. I've called the vet.'

He shot a glance in the horse's direction, and met Lucie's eyes. So they agreed on that, at least. Henry was in deep trouble. 'They're sending an air ambulance, because of the track. It should be here any minute. It was being scrambled from Wattisham airbase.'

She nodded. 'Good. The sooner the better.'

'I've just got to put out markers.' He ran down the field, opening out the sheets and spreading them in a rough H on the emerging crops. Moments later he was back, and knelt down opposite Lucie. 'Anything I can do? She needs a line in.'

'I know. Can you take over her neck so I can do it?'

'Sure.' His fingers slid around hers, cupping the fragile neck, and she eased her hand away carefully and then busied herself opening her bag and finding what she needed to get an intravenous line in. 'She needs saline.'

'They're bringing plenty of fluids. I told them to expect circulatory collapse.'

'Let's hope they get here soon,' Lucie said, checking Amanda's pulse and finding it weaker. 'Her pressure's dropping. Where the hell are they?'

'God knows, but the horse is going to be spooked by the helicopter.'

She'd got the line into Amanda's hand, and she taped the connector down and looked at Henry doubtfully. 'Can you lead him back to the stable?'

'Are you all right with her?'

'I'll manage. I don't need a terrified horse galloping over me.'

'I don't think he's galloping anywhere,' Will said softly, and she slid her fingers back under his and watched him as he went quietly up to Henry, speaking softly to him and holding out a reassuring hand.

The horse was shivering, clearly in shock himself, and Will led him slowly, hobbling on three legs, up the track and over the field towards the house.

He was back in no time, just as the helicopter came into view over the hill.

'That was quick.'

'I met up with the vet on the track. He's taken him on up,' he yelled, and then his voice was drowned out by the whop-whop-whop of the helicopter, and the grass was flattened all around them and Lucie ducked involuntarily.

Never mind spooking the horse, it didn't do a lot for her, but she was pleased to see it!

Seconds later the paramedic team was there, taking over from her, checking what had been done, getting fluids up and running, giving Amanda gas and air for pain relief and straightening her legs out to splint them, before putting on the spinal boards and lifting her into the ambulance.

Then they were away, and Will and Lucie stood watching the helicopter fade to a dot in the distance. 'I need to ring her mother—they'll have to talk to the vet and make decisions about Henry.'

'What did he hit? She said they hit something on the track.'

They walked back along it, and there, sticking up in the grass, was the end of a steel frame from a piece of redundant farm machinery. It had probably been there for ages, but this wasn't Will's land, and he didn't walk along this track often, he said.

It was just bad luck that Henry had gone so far over to the side, rather than sticking to the centre of the tracks, and it might have cost them both their lives.

Lucie shuddered. To think she'd just been envying them their headlong flight!

They went back to the house and found the vet in the stable with Henry, running his hands over the trembling horse and murmuring soothingly.

'How is he?' Will asked tautly.

'Shattered the cannon-bone of his off fore. It's not a clean break. They might be able to save it, but he'll never work again.'

'She's got insurance.'

The vet straightened up and met their eyes. 'I need to speak to his owners. My instinct is to shoot him now, but sentiment often gets in the way.'

'I'm sure they'd want him saved if possible,' Will said, and the vet nodded.

'I'll call Newmarket. They'll have to come and get

him. They have special transport with slings. He can't travel like this, he'll just fall over.'

He came into the house with them, and after Will had spoken to Amanda's parents and told them that Amanda was on her way to hospital, they confirmed that they wanted Henry saved if possible, and so the vet made several calls to set up the transport arrangements.

It seemed to be hours before Henry was loaded and away, the lorry picking its way infinitely slowly along the uneven track.

'I'm going to have to do something about that track,' Will said heavily, and turned away. 'I'm going to ring the hospital,' he said, and went into the house, leaving the door open as if he expected Lucie to follow. She did, sitting impatiently waiting until he finally got through to the right department. After a short exchange he replaced the receiver.

'She's in Theatre. She's got a pelvic fracture, both lower legs and right femur, and a crack in one of her cervical vertebrae, as well as cerebral contusions. Thank God she had her hat on, or she probably would have died of head injuries, but she'll be in for a long time, I think, judging by the sound of it. Her parents are both there, waiting for her to come round.'

Will glanced at his watch, or where his watch would have been, and swore softly before looking up at the clock. 'The day's nearly gone,' he said, and he sounded exasperated and irritable.

'I need another watch,' he went on. 'I don't suppose you feel like a trip to town, do you? I haven't bothered to get one till now because I couldn't wear it on that wrist, but I think the swelling's down enough now, especially if I get one with an adjust-able strap.'

'Sure,' she agreed. She wasn't sure how far she could walk. Her feet were rubbed raw after her long walk in the badly fitting wellies—not to mention run-ning up the field in them with her socks gathered up round her toes. Still, she'd manage. She wanted to be with him, if only so she could try and get their relationship back on an even keel after last night.

She didn't know what had happened to change his attitude, but something had, and if nothing else she wanted at least to go back to how they had been, instead of this icy and terrifying remoteness.

Will felt sick. Lucie was so sweet and open, almost as if Fergus was nothing. How could she be so fickle? He couldn't bear to think about it, so he closed his mind and tried to get back to how things had been, but it was hard.

Too hard.

He withdrew into an emotional safety zone, and then had to endure Lucie's puzzled looks for the rest of the day. He found a watch, the same as the one that he had smashed in his accident five weeks be-fore, and the saleslady was able to adjust it so it hung loosely on his still tender and swollen wrist.

'It's taking a long time to get back to normal,' Lucie said as they left the shop.

'I've been giving it a hard time,' he said shortly. 'I've had no choice, unless I resigned myself to total dependence, and I didn't have anyone to depend on.'

'You could have depended on me,' she said softly, and he gave a brief snort.

'I could. I would rather not.'

'So you've pushed your wrist too hard and probably damaged it more.'

'It's my wrist,' he said flatly, cutting off that line of conversation, and Lucie fell silent. He felt a heel, but he was having enough trouble with his own emotions, without worrying about hers. Damn Fergus, he thought, and had to consciously relax his hands because they were clenched into fists so tight both arms were rebelling.

'Let's go home,' he said, without bothering to ask her if there was anything she wanted to do in town, and then had a pang of guilt. She'd driven him there, after all. 'Unless you want something?'

She shook her head. 'No. We can go back.'

The journey was accomplished in silence, and when they got back she said she was going to sort a few things out and disappeared into the cottage. He let himself into the house, patted Bruno absently and checked the answering machine automatically.

Nothing. No distractions, nothing to take his mind off last night and Lucie's beautiful, willing body under his.

He slammed his fist down on the worktop and gasped with pain. Damn. He really, *really* had to stop abusing this wrist. He massaged it gingerly with the other hand, and could have cried with frustration.

'You're better off than Amanda,' he told himself, and decided he'd swap places with her in an instant if it gave him a chance with Lucie.

There was nothing, of course, to stop him competing with Fergus—except pride.

Fergus had a car that cost more than he earned in a year, flash clothes that would never have seen the inside of Marks and Spencer, and he'd stake his life that Fergus didn't live in a tumbledown, half-restored excuse for a farmhouse in the middle of nowhere, miles from the nearest habitation and out of range of a mobile phone transmitter!

There was no way he could compete with Fergus for the heart of a city girl, and he didn't intend to try. He'd just take last night as a one-off, the night that shouldn't have happened, and cherish the memory for the rest of his life.

He struggled unaided into the long veterinary glove, had a bath and then lit the fire, opened the Scotch and settled down for a night's indifferent television. Nothing could hold his attention—not drama, not talk shows, certainly not puerile comedy.

He was about to go to bed when the phone rang, and he got up to answer it, to find that it was Fergus.

'Could I speak to Lucie, please?' he said in his carefully modulated voice, and Will grunted and dropped the phone on the worktop in the kitchen, going across to the cottage in bare feet and rapping on the door.

Lucie opened it, looking bleary-eyed and sleepy, and he wanted to take her in his arms and rock her back to sleep. Instead, he glared at her. 'Fergus on the phone,' he snapped, and, turning on his heel, he strode across the yard, ignoring the sharp stones that stabbed into his feet.

Lucie followed him in and picked up the phone. Will didn't want to hear her talk to him. A huge lump of something solid was wedged in his chest, and he shut the door into the sitting room with unnecessary force and turned up the television.

'Fergus?' Lucie said, looking at the firmly shut door with dismay. 'What is it?'

'I miss you.'

'I know. Fergus, we've had this conversation a hundred times now. I can't do anything about it. We aren't right for each other.'

'How's Will?'

Sexy. Amazing. The most incredible lover, better than I could have imagined in my wildest dreams.

'He's all right.' Actually, she didn't know how he was. Short-tempered, but that was no surprise, he was usually short-tempered.

Except just recently, and last night.

Last night…

'Sorry, Fergus, you were saying?'

'I was asking if there's any chance for you with Will, or if there's any point in me coming up to see you tomorrow. I want to see you, Lucie. I want to ask you something.'

Oh, no. But, then again, maybe a little competition might sharpen up Will's act.

'Come for lunch,' she said. 'I'll see you at twelve.'

'OK. I'll bring something, don't cook.'

'OK. See you tomorrow.'

She hung up, contemplated the firmly slammed door and shrugged. Will could find out for himself that she was off the phone. She went back to her cottage, shut the curtains and curled up on the chair and howled.

She'd really thought they were getting somewhere, but this morning he'd been so unapproachable, and then he'd said that they shouldn't have made love last night!

How could he believe that? It had been the most beautiful experience of her life, and she didn't think she'd been alone, but there was more going on here than she understood. There had been pain in Will's eyes, a real pain that hinted at some deep and terrible hurt.

A woman in his past? Had he been terribly hurt by her, and was that why he didn't do the morning-after thing very well? Was it that he couldn't bear to confront his feelings, or had he—please, God, no—pretended she'd been the other woman? Had *that* been why he hadn't been able to look at her in the morning?

Lucie scrubbed at the tears on her cheeks, and stood up. Whatever, she couldn't get any closer to understanding him by thrashing it round and round in her head any more, and she might as well go to bed.

Except that the sheets carried the lingering traces of his aftershave.

She sat up in the midst of the crumpled sheets and took her diary on her lap. 'We made love last night,' she wrote. 'At least, I thought we did. Perhaps it was just amazing sex.'

A tear splashed on the page, and she brushed it angrily away. 'Fergus coming for lunch tomorrow. He wants to ask me something. Hope it isn't what I think it is. Amanda and Henry came to grief on the track by the river. Very dramatic. Thought we were going to lose them both, but apparently not. Oh, Will, I love you, but you drive me crazy. Why can't you just open up with me? I thought we had something really special, but it must have been wishful think-ing.'

She put the diary down, lay down in the middle of the crumpled bed and cried herself to sleep.

*   *   *

Fergus turned up at twelve. Will saw the car coming down the track from the end window in the house. He was struggling to strip the window, working with the wrong hand, and he paused and watched the car's slow progress. On second thoughts, maybe he wouldn't do anything about the track, and maybe Fergus would stop coming down.

He threw the stripping tool to the floor with a disgusted sigh, and shut the window, abandoning his hopeless task. He went down to the kitchen, arriving coincidentally as Fergus drew up, and he watched as Lucie came out to greet him with a kiss on the cheek.

Oh, well, at least it wasn't a full-flown no-holds-barred kiss of the sort he'd shared with her on Friday night. He should be thankful for small mercies—or perhaps Fergus was just too well bred to do it in public. He opened the boot of his car—a ridiculously small boot—and lifted out a wicker hamper.

If it hadn't hurt so much, Will would have laughed.

Game, set and match, he thought, and turned his back on them. He'd seen enough.

CHAPTER TEN

THE atmosphere between them remained strained over the next couple of days, but Lucie refused to let Will ruffle her, and by ignoring his moodiness it seemed to defuse it a little. At least, it brought a professional edge to their relationship, and for the first two days of the week it was all business.

Then, on Tuesday afternoon, he found her after her clinic and suggested visiting Dick and Pam. 'Dick's had his balloon angioplasty, and it's sort of on the way home. I thought it might be nice to pop in and see them.'

'And scrounge a couple of plants? You could take her back the pots from the others—they're lying dead by the back door, I noticed.'

'I know. I couldn't get them into the ground, and it's been dry,' he said shortly. 'You could have watered them.'

'I could have painted the outside of your house, but it's not in my job description,' she retorted, and put the cap back on her pen. 'Shall we go?'

'Only if you promise not to tell her they're dead.'

'As if I would.' She tossed the car keys in the air and looked at him expectantly. 'You coming, or walking?'

'Coming.' He stood up and headed for the door, holding it open for her so she had to brush past him. She felt him flinch and wanted to howl with frustration.

Why, when they'd been so close?

She drove to Dick's and Pam's in silence, pulling up outside the right white house this time, and she followed Will up the path and stood a little way behind him, admiring the front garden.

It had been five weeks since she'd first seen it, and now it was May, and everything was getting lush and starting to grow away. The bulbs were out, the daffodils finished but the tulips starting to nod their heads, growing up through the perennials that would soon rush up to swamp them.

So different from the boring, orderly town gardens she saw in London, which more often than not had a motorbike or car parked in them and a tattered fringe of forgotten vegetation round the edge.

She heard the door open, and then Will was hugging Pam, and she was smiling at Lucie and beckoning them in.

'Dick will be so delighted to see you—he's so much better. I'm amazed. He's back to work next week, and he certainly seems ready for it. The difference in him is incredible. He's in the garden, helping me with the daffodil leaves. Come and see him. I'll put the kettle on—can you stop?'

'Just for a short while,' Will agreed, arching a brow at Lucie, and she nodded.

'That's fine. A cup of tea would be lovely.'

They followed her through the house and found Dick bending over, tying off the tops of the daffodils, and as they went out he straightened up and beamed at them.

'Hello, there. Is this a social call?'

'It is, really. I just wanted to see how things were. I gather from Pam you're feeling much better.'

'I am, and it's all thanks to this young lady. My dear, I'm going to kiss you,' he announced, and, putting his hands on her shoulders, he planted a smacking kiss on her cheek. 'There. You're wonderful.'

Will shook his head and laughed. 'What did she say that I didn't?' he asked wryly, and Dick shrugged.

'Probably nothing, except you assumed I was afraid to die. Lucie here pointed out what a waste of my retirement it would be if I wasn't here to enjoy it, and I thought of the years I've paid into a pension just to let Pam sit back and squander it on a cruise, and I thought, Blow it, I'm going to do this! So there. That's all she said—just another angle on the same old theme, but it worked, and I can't tell you how grateful I am.'

Lucie laughed. 'Well, I'm delighted to have been of service. I must say, you do look well.'

'I am. Ah, look, here's Pam with the tea. Let's go and sit down in the conservatory.'

He led them up the garden, a riot of blue and yellow with the aubretia and alyssum foaming over the paths and tumbling down the walls, and they sat in the conservatory in the warm spring sunshine and talked about his operation, and how he'd felt, and they stayed far longer than they'd meant to.

Lucie didn't mind because as long as they were with Dick and Pam Will wasn't cold and remote.

Finally, though, he stood up to go, and on the way home he managed to keep the civilised veneer intact.

They got back as the phone was ringing, and he went in and came out again, calling her across the yard.

'Lucie? Phone—it's Fergus,' he said, and the coldness was back.

How odd. Surely it wasn't Fergus that was causing the problem, was it? Goodness knows. She went in, and as before he went through the door and closed it firmly in her face.

'Fergus?'

'Lucie, hi. How are things?'

She looked at the closed door. 'Just peachy, Fergus—just peachy,' she said heavily. 'How are you?'

Fergus again. Damn the man. Will looked morosely out of the window, staring at Henry's empty field. It seemed so odd without him. Apparently it was touch and go, but they were giving him time. Amanda, however, was making progress, and had recovered fully from her head injury. She would be in a neck brace for the next couple of weeks until her cervical fracture healed, and she had an external fixator on her pelvis to hold it, and her femur had been pinned and so had her lower legs, so that she didn't have heavy casts dragging her down once she started getting up and about.

Knowing how ruthless the physios were, Will thought it quite likely that she'd be up and about sooner than she thought or wanted, but he had it on good authority that she was a pretty tough cookie.

He wished he could drive. He wanted to go and see her, but he didn't want to ask Lucie. He was putting on her a lot, and he didn't want to—especially not now, when he was tortured by that night.

He could hear her voice speaking softly on the other side of the door, and, although he couldn't hear the words, every now and again she laughed, a soft, intimate little laugh that turned a knife in his gut.

He gulped and stared hard out of the window, down towards the river that would never be the same again since she'd been down there with him. Now he could see her there, outlined against the morning sky, her hair like a soft cloud around her head, and every time he went there he could feel her presence.

She hung up. He heard the clatter of the phone, and then her voice talking to Bruno, and then a tap on the door. 'Any news of Amanda?' she asked, coming through without waiting for the gruff invitation that was still locked in his throat.

'She's doing well. Everything's pinned and fixed and propped, and she's probably damned uncomfortable, but she's alive, and so is the horse, by a miracle.'

'That's good. I thought I might go and see her. I wondered if you wanted to come?'

Damn. She'd pre-empted him, and now he couldn't escape from her company, because he *did* want to see Amanda and it was more important than his personal feelings.

'I was thinking of going. I thought I'd get a taxi, to save you having to do all the running around.'

'I don't mind.'

So that was that. No way out, and anyway it would have been churlish. He snorted softly to himself. That didn't normally hold him back, he thought, and hated himself a little more.

They arrived at the hospital at seven, and Amanda, although obviously in pain still and very weary, was pleased to see them.

Lucie gave her some flowers to add to the many she already had, and Will showed her the card and hung it on a string over the bed with the others.

There was a cradle over her hips, keeping the bed-clothes off her fixators, and she was lying flat, of course, because of the neck injury, but she said the worst thing was the boredom.

'And it's only been a couple of days!' she wailed laughingly. 'What will I be like in a month?'

'Longing to lie down,' Will advised her. 'You wait till the physios get hold of you!'

'Oh, don't. There's one girl who's already having a go—she's lovely really, but she makes me do all sorts of things and it hurts! Still, it's my own fault. I shouldn't have been galloping along there on the verge. You don't know what it was he fell over, do you?'

'An iron bar, part of a bit of old farm machinery,' Will said. 'I've had a word with the farmer and he's moving it. He said he's very sorry to hear you had such a bad fall, but he pointed out it isn't an official bridleway.'

'Oops,' Amanda said with a grin. 'Oh, dear. My father was muttering about compensation. I'll have to talk him out of it!'

'Might be wise. Anyway, it's gone. Any news of Henry?'

'He's had an operation—they've splinted it with a bit of bone from a rib, and wired it all together, so goodness knows how he's managing to stand up, but he seems to be all right. They don't know how well he'll heal, but he seems to have settled down there, at least, and he's taking an interest in his surroundings. Of course, that's easier if you haven't got your neck wrapped in a plastic tube!'

They chatted a little longer, but then it was obvious that she was tiring, so they stood up to leave, and she reached out and took Will's hand. 'Thank you so much for helping me. They told me you saved my life, both of you, and I don't know what to say.'

Her eyes filled with tears, and Will bent and brushed his lips against hers. 'You don't have to say anything. I'll put it on your livery bill,' he said with a twisted little smile, and Lucie knew he was touched by her words.

She was, too, but she hardly knew Amanda. Will knew her all too well, and had spent months avoiding her. Odd, how he had now been cast in the role of hero.

Amanda held out her hand to Lucie, and she bent and kissed the girl's cheek. 'You take care, OK? We'll see you soon.'

They left her there, surrounded by her flowers and cards, and passed her parents on the way in. It meant another brief delay and another round of thanks, but then they were out and heading for the car.

'Fancy going to the pub for a meal? Or an Indian?'

She met his eyes, and wondered at his motive. Was this an attempt to mend fences, or would it be a chance to find out what had happened between Friday night and Saturday morning? Or was it simply that he was hungry and wanted to eat tonight?

Whatever, she was starving.

'Sounds fine. We'll do whatever you want—I'm easy.'

They went to an Indian restaurant, and discovered a shared passion for chicken korma in a really thick creamy sauce, with lots of twiddly bits to go with it and heaps of plain boiled rice, not the fancy pilau rice with spices, but just the clean, fresh flavour of basmati.

And Lucie wondered why it was that they could be so close in so many ways and yet she couldn't ask him what had happened and why he didn't want to talk to her after she'd given him her soul.

They didn't fight, though, and they kept the conversation trivial and away from anything that might damage the fragile truce that seemed to have sprung up between them.

And when they arrived back at the house, Lucie looked across at him and took a leap of faith. 'Coffee?' she offered, but to her relief and disappointment he shook his head.

'I won't. Thanks. I've got a couple of letters I ought to write and it takes ages with this stupid cast on. Maybe another night.'

'OK.'

She locked the car, handed him the keys and let herself into the cottage. Minnie was there, curled up on the bed, and she stretched and wandered out to the kitchen, asking for food.

'I don't do catfood, you'll have to speak to Will,' she told Minnie, and opened the door for her. Half an hour later she was back through the bedroom window, licking her lips, and curled up on Lucie's bed again.

Lucie was in bed herself, with her diary on her lap, telling it about Will and their meal.

'It was a really nice evening, but we were both walking on eggshells. What's happened? I must ring

Fergus tomorrow and give him an answer about those concert tickets for Saturday. Bet I forget.'

She did. She forgot on Wednesday, and so on Thursday morning, she stuck herself a note on the front of the fridge.

GIVE FERGUS AN ANSWER! it said, in big red letters, but she still forgot to ring him.

The truce with Will was still holding, and it really seemed as if they were about to make some progress. They got back from the surgery shortly before seven on Thursday evening, and on impulse she turned to him in the car and invited him in.

'Goodness knows what I've got, but you're welcome to it. I can probably throw something edible together.'

'OK,' he said cautiously. 'I'll just feed the dog and cat, and I'll be back.'

It took him a few minutes because he took Bruno for a run, but by the time he returned she'd thrown together a scratch supper with eggs and pasta and bacon, with a grating of cheese over the top.

'Perfect timing,' she said, handing it to him with a smile. It was gorgeous, and he sat there in the comfy armchair opposite her and wondered if she really felt that much about Fergus, or if there might be a chance for him.

Then Lucie got up to make coffee and he followed her through to the kitchen with his plate. 'Here, you can make the coffee, I'll wash up,' she suggested, and put the dishes in the sink while he started pottering with the mugs.

She'd tied her hair back in a scrunchie and he could see the nape of her neck, and he bent, unable to stop himself, and nuzzled it gently. 'I've got a better idea,' he murmured, and drew her into his arms. His kiss was gentle, nothing too demanding, but his pulse rocketed and his knees felt weak and it was like coming home.

'I tell you what, let's forget the coffee and the washing-up, shall we?' she suggested softly, and he smiled.

'I'll put the milk back,' he said, and then he saw the note. GIVE FERGUS AN ANSWER! With great care he put the milk in the fridge and shut the door, and turned to her, slamming down the pain and refusing to let it take control of him. Fergus again, he thought. And what answer?

'On second thoughts, maybe I'll have an early night,' he said, his voice sounding as if it came from miles away.

'What?'

'I—I can't stay. I'm not feeling all that good—my arm. I need some painkillers.'

'Is it all right if I come over and use the phone in a minute?' she said.

'Sure,' he agreed, and with great reserve he managed not to bolt for the door, hanging onto his control by a thread. Once he was in his kitchen he leant back against the door and banged his head against it firmly.

'Idiot,' he growled. 'How could you be so stupid? You know damn well Fergus is still after her.'

The door pushed behind him, and he moved away from it to let her in.

'Sorry, I was leaning on it, doing up my shoes,' he lied, and kicked them off anyway in favour of his boots. 'I'm walking the dog. Help yourself to the phone.'

'OK.' She dialled while he struggled into his boots, his right arm still too weak to pull hard enough, and then she started to speak before he had time to escape.

'Fergus? Hi, it's Lucie. The answer's yes.'

Will slammed the door behind him, taking the steps in one and veering onto the track at the end of the yard, heading down to the river at a run, Bruno at his heels.

Hell. What answer? *That* answer? Please, no, he thought, and ran faster, his legs pumping, his heart slamming against his ribs. Please, no, please, no, please…

Lucie hung up the phone, looked out of the window at Will heading down the track like a greyhound and shook her head. What the hell had got into him tonight—unless it was her ringing Fergus? He didn't seem to like it but, anyway, it had been before then.

She went back, cleared up her kitchen, watched television and then just before it was pitch dark she saw Will coming back, walking heavily as if he was exhausted.

Idiot. His arm would be playing up if he was treating it like that. She shut her curtains, went into the bedroom and turfed the cat off the pillow then went to bed with her diary.

I GIVE UP! she wrote. 'I can't rescue him, he's unrescuable. I'm going to London for the weekend, I've had enough. I told Fergus yes, so must meet up with him on Friday night. At least he's reliable and won't change his mind every ten seconds about whether he likes me or not.'

And throwing the diary on the floor, she settled

back and glared at the ceiling while it went slowly
out of focus and blurred. She blinked and it came
back into focus, but only for a second.

Damn. Not again!

She sniffed, pushed the cat out of the way again
and turned out the light. To hell with him. To hell
with all men. They were more trouble than they were
worth.

Except that this one, she knew, was worth ten of
any other man, and she couldn't seem to get through
to him.

Defeated, she let the tears fall, and in the morning
she packed her case, put it in her car ready, turned
the cat out and shut the windows. She'd come and
pick the car up after work, when she brought Will
back.

And then at least she'd have the weekend to cool
off before trying again.

If she could bring herself to try any more. Just at
the moment, she wasn't sure she could.

'Oh, Minnie, no! You are such a pain, cat. How did
you get in there?'

The cat mewed at him through the closed window,
and Will went into the house, fetched the spare keys
of the cottage and went back to let her out. She must
have darted in when Lucie left for London, he
thought, and a great heavy lump settled in his chest.

He might as well get used to it, though. He went
in through the cottage door, and Minnie ran into the
bedroom and jumped on the bed, settling down to
wash herself.

'You, little cat, are a nuisance,' he told her, and
scooped her up.

A book caught his eye, fallen open on the floor, and he sat on the edge of the bed and bent to pick it up. Then he froze, suddenly realising what it was.

A diary, written in Lucie's neat hand. Three words stood out in bold—RESCUING DR RYAN! Rescuing him? From what—apart from her? Oh, lord.

Slowly he picked it up and scanned the entry, guilt nudging at him, but he ignored it. She was writing about him, and somehow that made it seem less wrong. He read, 'He kissed me. Don't think he meant to. Don't think he means to do it again—we'll have to see about that! I have a feeling he needs rescuing from himself. It can be my next challenge—RESCU-ING DR RYAN!'

Rescuing me from myself? Am I so tragic? Yes, his honest self replied. Tragic and lonely and an object of pity. Oh, hell.

Will went on, flicking through the pages, scanning the odd entry until he arrived at last Saturday, almost a week ago. 'We made love last night,' she'd written. 'At least, I thought we did. Perhaps it was just amaz-ing sex.'

There was something so poignant about that that he felt tears fill his eyes. He blinked them away. There was a smudge on the page, as if it something wet had splashed on it and been brushed aside. One of Lucie's tears, to match his own? He swallowed hard and read on.

'Fergus coming for lunch tomorrow. He wants to ask me something. Hope it isn't what I think it is. Amanda and Henry came to grief on the track by the river. Very dramatic. Thought we were going to lose them both, but apparently not. Oh, Will, I love you, but you drive me crazy. Why can't you just open up with me? I thought we had something really special, but it must have been wishful thinking.'

I love you? *I love you?*

Oh, lord. He read on, but there was nothing very much. Comments on his temper, on their fragile truce, and then last night, after she'd phoned Fergus, she'd written, 'I GIVE UP! I can't rescue him, he's unrescuable.'

No, Lucie, Will's heart cried. Don't give up! I didn't know! Give me a chance. He read on, and horror filled him. 'I'm going to London for the weekend, I've had enough. I told Fergus yes, so must meet up with him on Friday night. At least he's reliable and won't change his mind every ten seconds about whether he likes me or not.'

Oh, lord. She'd given up on him, and gone to Fergus, and she'd told him yes. Yes to what? To sleeping with him? Living with him? Going back to London?

Marrying him?

'No,' he growled. Flinging the diary aside, he scooped up the startled cat and strode out of the cottage, locking it up and taking Bruno out to the kennel he used sometimes if Will was going to be out for long.

'Sorry, old boy,' he told him, giving him another bowl of food. 'I'll be back in the morning, whatever happens. On guard, eh, mate? Good lad.'

He shut the pen, and locked the house, throwing his light overnight bag in the car. He had to go via the surgery and pick up Lucie's address, but he'd already got Fergus's card which Lucie had pinned up on the board by the phone the other week and left there, so that would give him two places to start.

OK, he shouldn't be driving, but needs must, and he had to get to her before she did something irrevocable.

Like what? Sleep with him?

'We made love last night. At least I think we did. Perhaps it was just amazing sex.'

The very thought of Fergus touching her brought a surge of bile to his throat. 'She's mine,' he growled. 'She loves me, not you. Don't you lay a finger on her, you bastard!'

Will went up the track far faster than even the rugged Volvo was designed for, dodging the potholes whenever possible, and shot out onto the road with unwary haste. He picked her address up from her personnel file in the surgery, and then jumped back into the car and headed for the A12.

He needed a clear run and a following wind, and he got both, amazingly. He was in London in record time, probably picked up on scores of speed cameras, but he'd deal with that if and when it mattered. He cruised up and down, scanning the *A-Z* on his lap, and finally found her little street.

And there, right outside her address, was her car, squeezed into an impossibly tiny space. The nearest space he could find that he could fit the car in was three streets away in a residents' parking zone, but that was tough.

He slotted the car in, grabbed his bag and ran back to Lucie's, staring at the bells in puzzlement. This was her address—or it had been. Had she left it completely? He'd thought she'd handed it over to her flatmate, and still had a room here for emergencies. And maybe she was out with Fergus already—or up there with him.

His patience snapped, and he went for the right flat number, standing with his finger on the bell until he heard her voice on the intercom.

'Hello?' she said softly, and he felt suddenly sick with fear.

'Lucie, it's Will. Let me in.'

'Come on up. Third floor.'

The buzzer sounded, and he pushed the door open and ran up the stairs, his heart pounding, and there she was, standing in the doorway with a wary look on her face.

'Is everything all right?' she asked, and he pushed past her and swept through the flat, throwing the doors open, searching...

'Will?'

'Where is he?'

'Who?'

'Don't play games with me, Lucie. Fergus, of course. You said you were coming up here to see him. You said you'd see him on Friday.'

'No, I didn't.'

'Yes, you did, quite clearly—in your diary—'

'My *what*! You've been reading my *diary*?' She flew at him, her fists flailing, and he grabbed her wrists and held her still, wincing as she struggled.

'Yes, I've been reading your damn diary,' he growled. 'Only tonight, not before, but it was on the floor when I let the cat out, and I saw my name—'

'Where?'

'RESCUING DR RYAN. In capitals. And for your information, it wasn't just amazing sex,' he bellowed. 'We *did* make love.' His voice softened to a whisper. 'We did make love, Lucie—didn't we?'

Lucie looked up into his eyes, and her own filled with tears. 'I thought so.'

'You were right. It was just, with Fergus in the background, somehow it seemed wrong, making love to another man's woman—'

'Hey, hey, stop! I'm not Fergus's woman—'

'Don't go feminist on me, Lucie, you know what I mean.'

'Yes, I do,' she said, 'and I'm not. I'm not Fergus's woman! I've never slept with him—'

'Never?'

'No, never. I never will.'

He stared at her, stunned, unable to believe his ears. 'But...you said yes—didn't you?'

She frowned. 'Yes?'

'I don't know. You had to give him an answer.'

She started to laugh, and he let go of her hands and stalked across to the window, bracing his arm against the bar. His stomach was churning, and all she could do was laugh. 'It's not funny, Lucie,' he warned.

'Oh, Will, it is! He wanted to know if I wanted concert tickets for tonight. I said yes, but not for me, for my flatmate and her partner. That's where they are—they've gone to a rock concert in Hyde Park. He wanted me to go with him, but I wouldn't, so he offered me the tickets anyway. Said maybe I'd like to go with you.'

'He did?'

Will turned to face her, and she smiled and walked towards him. 'Uh-huh. He's on your side, Will. I can't imagine why, he's not into Neanderthal behaviour, but he's very magnanimous.'

'Witch,' Will muttered, and Lucie tutted and put her arms round him.

'Don't. No more fighting. I've had enough of it.'

'Me, too,' he said with feeling, and drew her closer. 'I love you, Lucie Compton,' he said softly. 'I'm sorry I didn't say so, but I really thought you were just toying with me, and Fergus was the love of your life, and I didn't want to make a fool of myself.'

'That stubborn pride of yours again,' she teased, and he groaned and dropped his head onto her shoulder.

'Very likely. Will you forgive me?'

She took his face in her hands and stared up at him, and her eyes were like luminous green pools. 'Oh, yes, Dr Ryan, I'll forgive you—just so long as you promise never to jump to conclusions again, and remember to tell me you love me at least three times a day, just so neither of us can forget.'

'You have to do the same.'

'Of course. I love you, I love you, I love you.' She smiled impishly. 'You're two behind.'

He kissed her, just the lightest brush of his lips. 'I love you,' he murmured, and kissed her again.

Then much later, after she'd agreed to marry him, he lifted his head and said again, 'I love you...'

MILLS & BOON®

Makes any time special™

Mills & Boon publish 29 new titles every month. Select from...

Modern Romance™   Tender Romance™

Sensual Romance™

Medical Romance™ Historical Romance™

MAT2

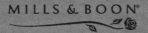

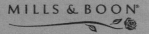

Medical Romance™

NURSE IN NEED by Alison Roberts

Emergency nurse Amy Brooks rushed into an engagement when she realised she wanted a family of her own—then she met Dr Tom Barlow. She had to end the engagement and Tom was delighted—but was his love for Amy the real reason?

THE GENTLE TOUCH by Margaret O'Neill

Jeremy is asked to persuade Veronica Lord into letting him treat her. Just as he gains her trust, Jeremy discovers that he was present when she had her accident and could have helped her. Will she ever be able to forgive him, let alone love him?

SAVING SUZANNAH by Abigail Gordon

Until Dr Lafe Hilliard found her, Suzannah Scott believed she had nothing left. Lafe helped her to rebuild her life and all he wanted in return was honesty. But if Suzannah revealed her past, she risked not only losing his professional respect, but his love…

On sale 4th May 2001

DAKOTA
BORN

Debbie Macomber
NEW YORK TIMES BESTSELLING AUTHOR

Lindsay's looking for a fresh start—and
Dakota holds the key to her past, and a
secret she's determined to uncover...

Published 20th April

0501/114/MB13

4 FREE
books and a surprise gift!

We would like to take this opportunity to thank you for reading this Mills & Boon® book by offering you the chance to take FOUR more specially selected titles from the Medical Romance™ series absolutely FREE! We're also making this offer to introduce you to the benefits of the Reader Service™—

    ★ FREE home delivery
    ★ FREE gifts and competitions
    ★ FREE monthly Newsletter
    ★ Exclusive Reader Service discounts
    ★ Books available before they're in the shops

Accepting these FREE books and gift places you under no obligation to buy, you may cancel at any time, even after receiving your free shipment. Simply complete your details below and return the entire page to the address below. *You don't even need a stamp!*

YES! Please send me 4 free Medical Romance books and a surprise gift. I understand that unless you hear from me, I will receive 6 superb new titles every month for just £2.49 each, postage and packing free. I am under no obligation to purchase any books and may cancel my subscription at any time. The free books and gift will be mine to keep in any case.

M1ZEA

Ms/Mrs/Miss/Mr ....Initials.......................................
                                                                 BLOCK CAPITALS PLEASE
Surname ....
Address ....
....
....Postcode....................................

Send this whole page to:
UK: FREEPOST CN81, Croydon, CR9 3WZ
EIRE: PO Box 4546, Kilcock, County Kildare (stamp required)